The Bother in

by

S. P. Moss

Circaidy Gregory Press

The Bother in Burmeon
Copyright information

paperback ISBN 978-1-906451-32-5
ebook ISBN 978-1-906451-55-4

Printed in the UK by
Berforts Group Ltd

Published by
Circaidy Gregory Press
Creative Media Centre
45 Robertson St, Hastings
Sussex TN34 1HL

www.circaidygregory.co.uk

Author's Note

The Bother in Burmeon is a work of fiction. Burmeon and Ybur are fictitious lands, and neither the characters nor the events in the story are intended to reflect the history of any actual countries.

While I have tried to be accurate in the technical aspects of the story, I hope that experts in this field will forgive a little poetic licence here and there.

For Johnny
by John Pudney

Do not despair

For Johnny-head-in-air;

He sleeps as sound

As Johnny underground.

Fetch out no shroud

For Johnny-in-the-cloud;

And keep your tears

For him in after years.

Better by far

For Johnny-the-bright-star,

To keep your head,

And see his children fed.

from "Selected Poems" by John Pudney, published 1946, The Bodley Head.

Contents

Chapter 1

The hunter and the hunted

His senses were on overdrive. His arms and legs were tickled by the crisp brown and white grasses of the Savannah. His mouth and nose breathed in the smell of wild honey, of sun-scorched leaves and of distant rain. A smell so intense that he could almost taste it. His ears buzzed with cicadas in their thousands, with the rustle of wind across the plains and with a low, faraway drumbeat.

If he kept his head down, he could see Ajay immediately ahead of him, also crouched, motionless but tensed, like a coiled spring in the dry grass. Ajay was well camouflaged in his khaki shirt and shorts but carried no weapon, only his trademark camera.

If he looked up, he could stare into the infinity of the East African sky, burning blue and awesome, making him feel as insignificant as one of the tiny ants that crept now around his bare knees.

Ajay turned his head briefly, raised his eyebrows and nodded. That was the signal that the lioness had been spotted and they were to move on. Silently, crouched like two cats, they crawled onwards to where the grass began to thin out and give way to a few gnarled bushes.

And then, in the buzz of the heat and the vibration of blue sky, he saw her, the lioness, also poised, and packed with the energy and the pulse of Africa. He saw her through the brown and white grasses, not five metres away from them. She was intent on something not five metres in front of her. This was amazing: who was the hunter and who was the hunted? Who, in the end, was stalking whom?

Chapter 2

The silver kaleidoscope

'Ker...pow!'

Billy had certainly not expected to be pounced on from behind. After all, the lioness had been some distance in front of him, in his line of view. He threw his arms back in wild surprise. The smell of Prawn Cocktail crisps on his attacker's breath swept his mind and body out of the savannah and back into an English classroom where he'd been gazing through the window into the early June greenness outside.

'Oh, pack it in, Josh!' Billy was annoyed that the most irritating boy in the class had invaded his daydream about his favourite TV program and dragged him back to reality. The reality of losing his pen yet again, that nasty bubble-gum he'd unwittingly trodden in and the less-than-glowing half term report that he was going to have to explain to Mum. It was bound to carry on with the same tedious theme of all his first year reports: "Billy must learn to concentrate on the here and now" and "Billy seems to be permanently lost in a dream." What was the problem with that, anyway? Teachers, parents and other grown-ups were continually trying to summon him back into *their* dreary world with silly phrases like "Anyone at

3

home?" or, worse still, by waving their hands backwards and forwards right in front of his eyes like windscreen wipers.

Now Josh had got in on the act, too. Josh was one of those boys who always went around with two others in tow, as if they'd all had an accident with the Superglue. Josh seemed incapable of ever amusing himself on his own for more than two seconds. He had to have his admiring mates around him, or to be fiddling with one of his many games and gadgets, or plonked in front of the TV watching *Darren does Danger* or some other rubbish.

'S'pose you were doing a brain overload of Ajay and his stupid adventures again...' Josh had let go of Billy, seeing his friend George, who had three big brothers, approaching.

'Well, yeah...and what's it to you?' Billy muttered, brushing down his hair. *Ajay's Adventures* was the one TV program that he really liked. Ajay was brilliant – he went round the world doing some really dangerous stuff and never used stuntmen or camera tricks. Ajay would be braving the rapids in Canada in a birch bark canoe that he'd built himself one week and living with an obscure tribe of tree people in the Amazon the next. Or stalking lions in the African savannah. He had a particular gift when it came to animals and seemed able to converse with them through some sixth sense.

4

Josh snorted a laugh that sprayed the remains of some chewed-up crisps onto Billy's collar. His two cronies sniggered.

'Ajay is sooooo totally pants! Dull, dull, dull! What's the point of something that calls itself an adventure without any special effects? And I don't believe old Ajay does all that stuff himself, either. I bet it's all fixed...give me *Darren does Danger* any day. Now *that's* cool. Daz the Danger Ranger. Yo!' Billy cringed as Josh did his impression of the dreadful Darren, a middle-aged man trapped in the clothes and expressions of a teenager.

'You're only saying that `cos Ajay's not on the right channel...like the one your darling Mummy used to read the news on...' Billy's friend George joined in.

'Oh yeah? Ajay is rubbish and that's official. I've heard he's going to be shown up for the cheat he is soon. I mean, look at him. No way does he do all that stuff for real. He must be at least as old as my granddad...or even Billy Blake's granddad...*if* he was still alive...'

If Josh wasn't boasting about his perfect family or playing with one of his electronic gadgets, then he was having a go at someone. Billy and George were this term's targets but they were proving quite resilient to Josh's teasing. Billy could drift off to another world, and George, because he was the youngest in a big family, had got very good at smart retorts. Billy didn't rise to the bait about the granddad comment so Josh tried another tack:

'So what *adventures* have you got lined up for the half term then, Billy Blake?' Josh wasn't interested in what Billy had to say. Billy knew that whatever he said would be used as an excuse to make some unfunny comment.

Billy decided on honesty. 'Oh, just staying with Gran,' he said.

'With Gran? Oh, yeah. Course. You haven't got any granddads, have you? I mean, not any more. Probably as well that they're dead. They'd be so totally *ancient* by now anyway. I'm off to stay with my nan *and* granddad for half term. In their villa. In the Algarve. That's in Portugal y'know. *My* granddad is really cool. He's got a super-mega-plasma-TV and a jacuzzi. D'you know what? The jacuzzi's got...' Josh blabbered on but one of the advantages of Billy's daydreamer attitude to life was that he could tune in to and, more importantly, tune out of this sort of waffle at will.

Billy knew all about Josh's granddad: Leslie de Winter. He was a huge, red-faced man who was always squeezed into polo shirts and slacks in unlikely colour combinations that looked as if they had been made for someone significantly younger and slimmer. Leslie de Winter was always slapping people on the back or crushing them around the shoulder while chortling and asking them to "Call me Les".

Billy groaned and turned to face George, blocking Josh out of view.

'You know where "Call-me-Les" can stick his jacuzzi! Wasn't that brilliant with Ajay and the lion...' George and Billy carried on excitedly talking about Ajay and their plans for summer half term. Frustrated, Josh and his cronies sloped off. Billy could hear muttering which rose to a louder chant of:

'Billy Blake

Tried to shout

Blew his nose

And his brain fell out!'

'I hear it's tipping it down in the Algarve!' George yelled back. He turned to Billy: 'Bet you'll have a brill time at your gran's!'

Billy grinned at his friend. 'Yeah...I will, George. It's gonna be...I dunno...' he looked out of the window up at the sky. 'It just is. I know!'

Billy sometimes wondered what it must be like to be part of a big, noisy family like George's. Or even to be part of the perfect de Winter "World's best granddad/ mum/sister" tribe. His own family was very small indeed. There was only Billy, his mum and dad, and it was a rare occasion that they were all together at home.

Billy's mum did something called freelancing which meant that she was always dashing off here or rushing off there, with the odd week working at home in between. It also meant that Mum was always apologising for all the dashing and rushing and just about everything else under the sun, too. Billy's mum said sorry for not being there. She said sorry for being there but being too busy. She said sorry for being old and grumpy. She said sorry for Billy not having brothers and sisters. Billy wasn't really bothered by any of the things that Mum apologised for. She was not really grumpy, except when she had too much freelancing to do or when her camera or computer broke down. And when Mum wasn't there, Billy got to go and stay with Gran.

Gran was Mum's mother. Although she lived just a few miles away, she seemed to live in another world. There was simply more *time* in Gran's world. Nothing was run by the clock. You never *had* to be here, there or anywhere by this or

8

that time. There was time to gaze out of the window and daydream. Gran's house and garden were full of solid, lasting things like dark wood cupboards and big pine trees. There were certainly no super-mega-plasma-TVs or jacuzzis.

Gran's husband had died just a few weeks before Billy was born. Mum always told Billy that, when Billy was still in her tummy, she had asked her father what he'd like to be called by his grandchild.

'Grandpop,' he'd said.

So Billy knew his grandfather as Grandpop. Grandpop had been a pilot in the RAF. Gran had a big black and white photo of him in the sitting room. There were paintings of the planes he used to fly dotted around her house: up the stairs and on landings and in the study. In photos, Grandpop was always in uniform. Billy could not picture him in a pink polo shirt and pair of banana yellow slacks, like "Call-me-Les." Thankfully.

The sun was high in a glorious June sky that promised a perfect half term as the children waited by the school gates to be collected. George and Billy normally went on the bus but today was special. George's oldest brother had just passed his driving test and was going to be picking him up. Billy's mum was coming to take him to Gran's in between dashing here and rushing there.

Billy and George looked up from scrabbling around with sticks in the roots of the pine tree by the gates. A huge silver thing invaded their field of vision and came to a noisy halt directly in front of the school gates. "Call-me-Les", resplendent in white pirate-style trousers and a turquoise striped shirt, dismounted theatrically from the shiny 4X4 and boomed out, to the whole school, it seemed:

'Well, what do you know, Joshua? If it isn't your old granddad come to whisk you off to Villa de Winter! Your mum wanted to come herself but I thought – safety first – women drivers and all that – leave it to Les!' He chortled as Josh sauntered, beaming, through the gates to receive a hefty slap on the back.

Billy shook his head. George rolled his eyes and grimaced but then jabbed Billy in the ribs with his stick and pointed, shrieking with laughter at the scene unfolding on the road outside. "Call-me-Les" and Josh had clambered into the huge 4X4 but Les was now evidently having trouble re-starting the beast. It sat, spluttering and completely blocking the school entrance. A number of other cars were now stuck behind it, led by an ancient VW Beetle convertible, as blue as the summer sky, filled with George's brothers. As the hooting increased, Les grew redder in the face. He shouted into his mobile phone and fiddled with the key in the ignition:

'You should get a better car, mate!' George's brother yelled out, laughing. 'Something a bit more modern and reliable!' But it was unlikely that Les heard him above the air conditioning as he eventually got the monster started and stormed off en route to Villa de Winter and its gadgets.

George waved goodbye and ran up to the little Beetle. He vaulted into the back seat on top of a brother, who protested loudly as the bundle of boys and car drove off into the sunshine. There were very few children left now, just Billy and a handful of girls sitting on the wall, giggling over some secret scraps of paper. As the girls were collected, sliding down and laughing as they piled into a big comfortable-looking car driven by a big comfortable-looking woman, Billy felt a pang of loneliness and a slight twinge of something like envy. But that was swept aside as his mum rushed up, short of breath:

'Oh, Billy, I'm so, so sorry I'm late again! Oh my God! You're the last one here...oh, you poor boy...come here, give me a hug...I was in such a rush...I'm dashing off at the crack of whatsit tomorrow to Jersey so we can catch the light for the shoot...it's marvellous at this time of year...and then there was total panic about the camera cable…I thought it had ended up in the washing machine…and then your bag…'

Billy smiled as he climbed into the rather tatty car with its mess of sweet papers, Mum's shoes and photography magazines. Mum continued her non-stop babble as Billy sat back and watched the school disappear into the distance:

'…I had to pack it and unpack it at least six times and then the phone went, and it was that complete twerp Art Director from the agency and then I nearly forgot your rucksack…'

Mum's replay of the mad panics, quick dashes and manic rushes that had happened just in the last hour faded into the background as they drove. Billy felt a sense of time slowing down as the car found its way through tree-lined avenues to Gran's house.

The first you saw of Gran's house were two curvy signs on either side of the drive, nestling amongst rhododendrons that bloomed deep crimson and honey purple in early summer. On the signs was the name of Gran's house: *Pinemount*. A short driveway led to a white house with green window frames. Billy could smell roses and honeysuckle as he climbed out of the car onto the gravel drive.

12

Gran appeared from the side of the house with a wooden trug basket full of weeds and deadheads. Gran never made stupid comments about how Billy had grown (it would be a bit odd if he didn't grow) or press sweets into his hand then ignore him for the rest of the visit, like other grown-ups. Instead, she walked over to him and shook his hand. Then she hugged him and said:

'Billy – I can't tell you how much I've been looking forward to your visit!'

They went in and had tea in the sitting-room, surrounded by the paintings of Grandpop's planes – a Sunderland flying boat, a Chipmunk training plane and a Hawker Hunter jet. For tea were slices of Battenberg cake on china plates with a pattern of cherry trees in blossom. Mid-cake, Billy glanced over at the black and white photo of Grandpop. Was it a trick of the light or were his eyes twinkling?

'Well, Billy. Do you want to take your bag up to your room? You know the way.'

Josh was always boasting that his house had three bathrooms, which it may well have done, but it only had one staircase, straight up the middle of the house. Gran's house only had one bathroom, which was tiny, and a downstairs loo, which was always freezing cold, even in summer, but there were two staircases. One was quite grand and in the middle of the house and the other was small and steep and at the side. Billy went up the middle staircase with his bag to what had been Mum's room when she was a girl. Half way up, his nose twitched. Mixed with the smell of honeysuckle that crept in from the landing window was another smell. A smell that Billy didn't recognise because it came from another age. Something smoky, but sweet.

Mum's old room was at the back of the house. The window looked out onto the back garden, a long stretch of lawn ending in a small wood of oak and pine trees. The room hadn't changed much since Mum had left it all those years ago. There was a green laundry basket at the foot of the bed that Gran called the toy box and a couple of fading camel stools with bells and tassels. Billy dumped his bag on the bed and made his way down the other staircase, the narrow one at the side of the house. This time a hint of another sort of smell drifted by – the way newly polished shoes would smell. Billy heard a faint *tap, tap, tap* on the stairs behind him and turned around. But there was nothing to be seen except the small open window and an early summer sky.

Once Mum had rushed off in a panic about whether the radio alarm was going to work at the crack of whatsit tomorrow, Gran and Billy could relax. There was no dashing, leaping or flapping to be done unless you really wanted to. The two of them spent a very pleasant evening building and burning a bonfire in a clearing in the woods. With the smell of fire still in their nostrils, they sat in the conservatory at the back of the house until dusk and darkness came.

Billy chose the middle staircase to go up to bed and paused again by the open window to breathe in the smell of night honeysuckle. He caught a faint whiff of smoke but was so weary that he assumed it was from the bonfire. Tired and happy, he changed into his pyjamas, brushed his teeth and slipped into bed. He closed his eyes and fell asleep almost immediately, his thoughts full of bonfires and aeroplanes.

What seemed like just seconds later, Billy woke and sat up in bed. It was dark in the room but a light shone through from outside. He got onto his knees and drew back the curtain.

Outside, the full moon shone almost as bright as day. He peered out on the garden. The lawn and pine trees were bathed in moonlight and everything looked dark green and silver. Billy had no idea what time it was or why he was looking out of the window. But he was completely spellbound and just had to stare at how beautiful it all was. He heard faint noises. The sound could have been the rustle of the wind in the trees or it could have been the sound of an engine or propeller, far away. An indescribable feeling of excitement clutched at him, as if something wonderful was just about to happen.

Billy fell into a dream. It was a weird, mixed-up dream about floating and falling and flying through a giant tunnel with ever-changing shapes and patterns on its sides, in colours of dark green and silver.

When he woke again, sunlight was streaming through the curtains instead of moonlight. He looked outside and normal colour was resumed in the back garden. When Gran asked him at breakfast if he had slept well, Billy said he wasn't sure. Gran just smiled and said that only very dull and boring people sleep soundly through a full moon.

That day, Gran busied herself around the garden while Billy checked in and out of the house seeing if all was as he remembered. In the same way that a cat likes to keep a territory of his own, which he inspects and prowls regularly, so was it with Billy at Gran's. He had to see if his legs were long enough yet to climb up between the two closest oak trees in a sitting position. He had to check out whether the huge board with the railway track on it was still resting on two planks at the top of the garage. He had to find the key of what Gran called the cocktail cabinet and open it to breathe in the delicious mix of aromas. But none of this was like the compulsion of having to be at judo at five precisely or having to get to the next level of the latest game before George did.

'Have you looked inside the toy box yet?' Gran sat in the conservatory, sipping a gin and tonic as the sun went down over the pine trees. 'You always seem to find something of interest in there. Your grandpop brought things back from his travels for the children when they were small. Odd little presents from all those places where he was stationed. The children were so thrilled when he came home…he always had some curio or other with him…and stories to tell, of course.'

'D'you know?' said Billy, grinning. 'I was just thinking it was time for a look…'

'You go ahead, Billy. I'm sure you'll sniff out something special there!' Gran smiled, mysteriously.

Twilight is a strange time. The air thickens somehow and time seems to hang there, trapped like a fly in a spider's web. Billy was not sure whether to put the light on in his room or not. He decided against it. The toy box with its padded top and "Lloyd Loom" sign sat at the end of the bed. He lifted up the lid and peered in. There were a few things on top that he knew and remembered – a plastic crocodile with snapping jaws, a collection of tiny Second World War soldiers and a few flat-looking creatures with matted neon hair that Gran called gonks.

Billy picked all these things out, rather impatiently, and rummaged around for something new. His hand met a cylindrical thing. He pulled it out. Now, this was something he hadn't exactly seen before but it seemed oddly familiar. It was a silver cylinder that he knew was a kaleidoscope. He admired the engraving of a splendid Indian goddess riding on a tiger. Then, he held the kaleidoscope up to his eye and turned the cylinder around. Jewel-like fragments filled with light and formed themselves into intricate symmetrical patterns. Billy turned the cylinder again and the little pieces of sapphire blue, ruby red and emerald green turned and somersaulted into another snowflake-like array. The bright specks were like those little coloured lights that float past your eyes as you're trying to get off to sleep, which Billy had always tried to catch when he was younger. Another turn and the snowflake was gone forever, rapidly transforming into something equally beautiful but totally different as the tiny jewel fragments spun and tumbled into place.

Billy's attention wandered from the everyday world: he became lost in the kaleidoscope with its perpetual possibilities and its magic micro-world of dancing jewels. And, as he watched the pattern before him slowly forming into a tiger's face, with stripes of amber and emerald eyes, he became aware that there was someone else in the room. Billy's nose noticed the stranger first – that sweet, smoky smell and the freshly polished shoes. A smell from another age.

'Great Scott! Where on earth have I landed up? Good God! It can't be...but how the dickens did those blessed pine trees get so tall?'

Billy looked up and refocused. A man stood there, gazing out of the window at the dusk-covered lawn, as if he'd emerged from the thick twilight air. He was a very handsome man with short brown hair, younger than Billy's Dad. He looked like someone from an old James Bond film; pipe in hand, shaking his head as he stared, bemused, at the darkening garden outside. Billy knew exactly who the man was. He was overcome with a mixture of awe, fear and guilt. Had he somehow been responsible for conjuring him up?

'Hmm!' The man looked from left to right through the window, one eyebrow raised in slight bewilderment. As if to solve the puzzle, he turned briskly to Billy, stretched out his right hand and spoke in a military, but not unfriendly, tone:

'Squadron Leader Walker, RAF.'

Billy was totally perplexed as to what to do. The polite part of him started to put out his hand to shake, as he knew he should. But he was scared and reluctant about touching what could only be a ghost. He scratched his ear with the hand he'd half put out and stared at the man intently. He looked real enough. He was not a particularly tall man but there was something very neat and dapper about him. He was just the right size to fit in a plane without any gangly legs or arms falling out anywhere.

'Um...this is a bit difficult,' Billy really didn't know what to say. 'I...um...*do* know who you are...'

'Well, that gives you an advantage over me, anyway, old chap. I haven't the foggiest who *you* are. Now, I think I know *where* I am, but as for when...and for that matter, how? Then again, I wouldn't put anything past the boffins these days...if we're sending men into space, then I suppose it's just possible...but maybe you can help. How would it be if we start with name, rank and number...as it were,' he added with a chummy smile, seeing Billy's discomfort.

'Well, my name's Billy Blake, and this is my gran's house...'

'Your gran! Good heavens! One generation further than I thought...'

'Yes,' Billy ventured. 'I think you must be my grandpop...'

'Grandpop?' The man puffed on his pipe and narrowed his eyebrows, as if rapidly thinking through the consequences of this bizarre situation. 'Not sure if I'm ready to be a grandpop – after all, I'm not even a daddy yet but I suppose...let's shake on it, Billy. Delighted to meet you!' Grandpop took the pipe out of his mouth and stretched out his right hand again. But Billy was still reluctant.

'Um...Grandpop...look, I'm really sorry and I don't want to be rude but aren't you, I mean, aren't you supposed to be...you know...'

'Dead, do you mean?' Grandpop put his right hand back by his side and the pipe back in his mouth. He puffed on it, thoughtfully. 'Everything is relative, old chap. You see, I could refuse to shake *your* hand on the basis that you're not supposed to have been born yet.'

'Well, no, I mean, no, I'm not refusing to shake your hand or anything,' Billy could feel himself going red and thrust out his hand to grab Grandpop's. The handshake was warm and firm.

'That's the boy! Dead, eh? Hmm...er...' Had Grandpop's cheeks coloured slightly? 'Your "Gran" doing well, is she?' Billy nodded enthusiastically as Grandpop continued. 'And how did I...' he shook his head and shuddered: '...no, no, more information than need to know. Yes, when my time comes, I just want to make a quick exit. Fly west...now, what are we going to do about this little pickle we find ourselves in?'

'Pickle?'

'Yes, pickle! I was busy preparing for a mission – got a spot of bother in the jungle – when I seemed to be catapulted forward into God knows when in the future. I would quite like to get back and, no doubt, having met me and shaken hands and all that, you'd rather not have a Grandpop who's meant to be...to have flown west lurking around your bedroom. How *did* you conjure me up, old chap?'

'Um...I don't really know if I did...you see, I was looking at this kaleidoscope here...I think you must have brought it back from somewhere for my mum...when she was little, I mean...' Billy showed Grandpop the kaleidoscope. Grandpop held it up and admired the craftsmanship and the engraving of the goddess and tiger. He shook his head and handed it back:

'Never seen the thing in my life. Although it does have the mark of a certain Flight Sergeant I know about it!'

Billy carried on. 'Well, I was looking into it and making different patterns and suddenly there was a tiger face…and you popped up. I was just looking into it like this…' Billy put the kaleidoscope up to his eye, closed the other and twisted the shaft around. 'It's brill – it makes all sorts of different patterns, and some of them even look like things, like there's a snake…a hooded cobra or something…here, Grandpop, have a look…'

But when Billy took the kaleidoscope from his eye to hand it to Grandpop, Grandpop had disappeared. Only a very faint whiff of pipe smoke lingered in the air.

Chapter 3

An E-Type Jag

Billy slept as soundly as a bear in winter that night. In fact, he slept right on until after nine the next morning, when it had already been light for hours. He was woken by a ringing sound and was vaguely aware of Gran's voice downstairs. He stretched out in bed, comfortably; then his still-sleepy eyes met with the kaleidoscope, on the carpet where he must have left it last night. What *was* all that about? In some ways it should have felt eerie and scary, a man who was meant to have been dead for twelve years just appearing like that – and looking as he must have done some time in the 1960s – but Billy simply didn't feel scared. In other ways it had all seemed like the most normal and natural thing in the world to happen.

At breakfast, Billy could have sworn that Gran was giving him a quizzical look. He was still not sure whether that had all really happened or whether it was some weird but incredibly vivid dream. It wouldn't be the first time he'd had one of those. But, if Grandpop really was a ghost, that could be really upsetting for Gran. She had been married to him for over forty years, after all. So Billy said nothing.

Then Gran said: 'I don't know if you heard anything while you were in bed,' Billy shook his head violently. 'But that was your mum on the phone. Everything is fine and she sends you a big hug and kiss but she was in a little bit of a panic about a camera. Her small camera, she said. The one she makes test shots on. Anyway, she seems to have mislaid it somewhere and wondered if you had seen it.'

Relieved that the subject was mislaid cameras and not dead grandpops, Billy attempted to be helpful:

'Um...d'you know? It might be in my bag. I know Mum was packing my bag and hers at the same time and she was in a bit of a tiz about some bit of cable. P'raps the camera ended up in the wrong bag? I'll have a look...'

'Well, finish your breakfast first.... I'm sure it won't be a total catastrophe if we don't ring your mum back at this very moment.'

Billy wasn't so sure, knowing Mum and her panics, so both he and Gran were relieved when he found the camera. It was in his rucksack, which he'd dumped in the hallway, beneath a painting of a Sunderland taking off from a turquoise-coloured lagoon. Billy's view of the world was that there was always a reason for missing things to turn up when and where they did, even if it wasn't always immediately obvious why.

Gran mentioned to Billy that she had to do something with the flowers over at the church and would he be able to amuse himself alone for a couple of hours? When Gran left, Billy began to get a fluttery feeling in his tummy. He realised that as long as there was breakfast, Gran to talk to and the camera to be found, he could stay downstairs and avoid what was lying on his bedroom carpet. But now that Gran was out of the house, he had no excuse. He absent-mindedly picked his rucksack up from the camel stool and put it on his back. Still avoiding the stairs, he gazed at the picture of the flying boat. What *had* he unwittingly unleashed? Was Grandpop a ghost? Shouldn't he be frightened? But then came a fear of another sort: what if it *was* all a figment of his imagination? What if he were to look into the kaleidoscope again and nothing, absolutely nothing was to happen? There was no choice. He had to find out. He tore up the main stairs to his bedroom.

The kaleidoscope was lying on the rug where he'd left it. Billy grabbed it. His mouth was dry and his heart pounding. The cold metal against his eye contrasted with the heat of the June sunshine streaming through the windows. Outside, bees were buzzing in the lavender. He heard the faint hum of a distant lawnmower. He turned the kaleidoscope shaft at first with nervous excitement but then increasingly with frustration as the dancing jewels formed themselves into one abstract pattern after another. He took the thing away from his eye and shook it violently. He looked with the other eye. He made short turns. He made long turns. He kept both eyes shut for a count of five after each turn. What was the trick? How did he get the tiger? And then he sat on his bed, rucksack still on his back, momentarily defeated. He held the kaleidoscope in his palms and stroked the engraving of the tiger with his thumb:

'Please, tiger…please…come again…just once more!' Billy whispered and slowly put the cylinder to his eye. He turned the shaft with both eyes closed, stopped and waited:

'Please!'

Billy opened his right eye. He was staring into a face this time. But it wasn't the tiger. It was a snake with ruby red eyes and a flashing tongue: the cobra he had seen last night just as Grandpop had disappeared into thin air. And then Billy experienced a most curious sensation. He felt his feet sliding away from under him and his body started turning, floating, weightless in space. The ruby eyes of the cobra flickered and disintegrated into thousands of glittering pieces as Billy fell and turned. He caught a faint whiff of that pipe smoke, and of the lavender from outside.

Billy felt himself whirling and turning down and round in a strange tunnel. The sensation was a mixture of that feeling you get when you're just about to drop off to sleep and that of being spun around in one of those giant teacups at the amusement park. He was aware of vague sounds – a dog yapping, someone whistling a song from long ago and the *pfft pfft pfft* of an old car.

Billy wasn't too sure what was going on with his eyes. Every now and then he'd catch a glimpse of something: a polished hubcap, a furry leg, a stripy cravat. But before anything real materialised, everything would turn into the shiny jewel fragments of the kaleidoscope and he'd turn and float and whirl down in another direction.

There were smells, too. The smell of newly mown grass, the smell of Castrol R, the smell of Old Spice and the smell of leather seats. It was actually the smell of motoring on a summer afternoon fifty years ago but Billy wouldn't have known that.

Gradually, Billy sensed that he was slowing down, or, at least, that he was back in three dimensions rather than about ten. The hairs on his bare arms stood up, as if he'd come into a cool room from the summer sunshine. And the smells changed subtly, too: his nose became aware of something like pear drops or some other long-forgotten boiled sweets. The jewel pieces drifted into the background. Real objects from wherever he was going to land began to take on an air of solidity: a dark wooden counter, packets of food in cheerful primary colours and a substantial set of scales with black iron weights.

Billy landed just inside the door of a little old grocer's shop. It was a calm and inviting place in comparison to the horror of Tesbury's, the huge supermarket on the outskirts of town that Mum dragged him along to every week. Behind the counter stood an array of tins, jars and packets: custard powder next to Mulligatawny soup; Lemon Curd next to Fray Bentos steak and kidney pie. A comforting smell of fresh ham and brown paper bags tickled at his nose.

A friendly looking man wearing a grey coat and owlish glasses stood beaming behind a bread-crumbed leg of ham. Billy could only see the back of the grocer's customer – a white shirt and a glimpse of a stripy cravat – but he knew straight away from the man's military bearing and clipped but exceedingly polite manner of speaking who he was.

'Ah, Mr Green. A very good day to you. I need a few provisions if you'd be so kind. Would you have a tin of Peek Frean's Afternoon Tea Assorted – they're a bit scarce in the jungle, it seems? Jolly good. And...fish paste, two jars. And...'

Grandpop puffed on his pipe thoughtfully. 'Yes, I suppose I should stock up on the old baccy. The usual, if you please. Two packets should see me to the next NAAFI...'

'Certainly, Squadron Leader. You'll be on your way to Bigglesbrook, no doubt. A marvellous day for it, if I may say so. Anything else you'd like, Squadron Leader...oh, good day, young man...' Mr Green looked up from the counter to where Billy was hovering in the doorway. Grandpop turned, raised his eyebrows and gave Billy a look of amused annoyance.

'Billy, old chap! Where on earth did you parachute in from?'

'Grandp...' Billy began but Grandpop coolly turned back to the grocer. 'Mr Green. Billy is a young...er... relative of mine. I think a quarter of *gobstoppers*...' he pronounced the word slowly, turning to Billy '...wouldn't go amiss at this point. Then we really must get cracking. This young chap needs to get back to his gran. How much do we owe you, then?'

Mr Green didn't have a scanning machine or an electronic till. He totted the sum up quickly, in his head. 'That will be eight-and-seven pence ha'penny.'

'Thank you, Mr Green and good day to you!' Grandpop paid with some strange little coins and got some strange big

30

coins back as change. While Grandpop didn't literally take Billy by the ear and march him outside, that was rather the feeling that he got as Grandpop ushered him through the shop door and out into the bright sunlight. Billy squinted as he stared up at the shop sign: *Forget-me-not Stores.*

'Now then, what the blazes do you think you're playing at?' Grandpop demanded. 'Come on,' he lightened his tone as he saw Billy's alarmed expression 'that jape you sprung on me yesterday evening was one thing but I'm just about to set off on an important mission and I'm in no mood for this sort of tom-foolery. Now, I'd suggest that you get your time travel tube or whatever it was that you showed me last night and get back – or forward if you must – to whichever century you belong in.'

'But Grandpop,' Billy stuttered, 'I don't honestly know if I can. You see, the kaleidoscope...I'll have a look, but...' He took the rucksack from his back and started rummaging through it.

'Now, I really don't have time for any more of this nonsense. I may be from the last century, as far as you're concerned, but I'm not a complete cloth-head. I can well imagine that fooling around with time and space is exactly what young chaps from the future get up to...I was quite content to play with my railway set at your age... but I suppose the world must progress...and I really must be on my way now.'

Billy had located some bits of string, a stick in the shape of a pistol and, incongruously enough, Mum's digital camera in the rucksack. But no kaleidoscope. He began to panic. Here he was, trapped in another world, with a ludicrously young Grandpop who thought he was messing around and was about to desert him.

'Please, Grandpop,' Billy felt tears welling up. 'Honestly, honestly... I don't know how to get back. That kaleidoscope...I only saw it for the first time yesterday...and now it's gone...please help me!'

Grandpop took one look at Billy's worried face and sighed, smiling. He ruffled Billy's hair:

'Well, old chap, I think I'm going to have to do the decent thing. You'd better come with me. Don't worry; we'll get you back somehow – something will turn up. Now, come and meet Monty!'

Billy walked with Grandpop down the sandy lane to where a little frog-eyed green sports car was parked, smiling a chrome smile. A lively fox terrier leapt out of the passenger seat and greeted Grandpop and then Billy enthusiastically, all paws and tongue.

'Hello, Monty!' Billy rubbed the dog's ears and Monty gave him a big wet lick, which tickled. Billy laughed. 'Ace car, Grandpop! What is it?'

'Austin Healey Sprite...fine little motor,' Grandpop beamed. 'And she's going to take us all the way to Bigglesbrook if you're game. You'll have to squeeze in with Monty at the front but it looks as if you're chums already so that shouldn't be a problem. So... chocks away to Bigglesbrook. Roger?'

'My name's Billy, actually...'

Grandpop flung Billy a bit of a look and then grinned. The prospect of a ride in the Austin Healey, the reassuring feel of Monty beside him and a deep knowledge, from somewhere, that with Grandpop he'd be all right, chased the worries out of Billy's head. He'd go along for the ride, as it were.

The car started up with a *pfft pfft pfft* as Grandpop reached for his gold-rimmed sunglasses. He somehow managed to drive, smoke his pipe, prevent Monty from leaping out of the car and accept the presence of his grandson from the next century all at the same time.

'Is there a seat belt or something?' Billy fumbled around by his shoulder.

'Goodness me, no. I'm quite capable of handling this motor – after all, I'm normally operating in three dimensions when I'm up in the air…'

As the Austin Healey gained speed, Billy felt dangerously close to the ground. Every stone or small pothole in the road became exaggerated. But soon his fear was overtaken by exhilaration as he felt the early summer breeze against his face and Monty's warm curly coat under his fingers.

'This is brilliant!' he yelled at Grandpop.

'Just wait 'til we go flying!' Grandpop grinned back. 'Now that the provisions are taken care of, how about a cup of char in half an hour or so?' Seeing Billy's confused expression he added hastily 'or a sticky bun or something.'

'A sticky bun sounds good.' Billy was beginning to feel a little peckish – breakfast had been decades ago… or perhaps hadn't happened yet.

'Terrific. Here's a gobstopper to be getting on with – then it's full steam ahead to the Lupin Tea Rooms.'

Billy leaned back, enjoying the sun and wind on his face. He felt so close to the road, so close to the engine and so close to the hedges. The roads all seemed narrower than they should be, framed by hawthorn and clumps of Queen Anne's lace. The Sprite hopped over hump-backed bridges where there was only room for one car – and a small one at that. It meandered past village greens with cricket pavilions and pubs with hanging baskets. They even hit a ford at speed. Cooling water splashed against Billy's warm skin.

Some of the villages they passed through seemed vaguely familiar but they were smaller, compacter, prettier, without the garish signs for McDonald's, Tesbury's or DIY centres. Something else was odd. There were hardly any other cars on the road. While the Austin Healey was travelling at quite a pace, the rest of the world seemed to be having a summer afternoon nap, as if suspended in a hammock.

Only one other road-user stuck in Billy's mind: as they drew up to a level crossing, a car approached from the other direction and screamed through the gates just as they were closing. It was a sleek and evil-looking E-Type Jaguar with a rather sleek and evil-looking man at the wheel. Billy shuddered involuntarily and cuddled up to Monty's reassuringly warm coat.

'Blithering idiot!' Grandpop shook his fist at the driver but the car was long past them.

Their journey took them to a filling station called National Benzole and next to it, the Lupin Tea Rooms. A large painted wooden sign announced "Teas & Refreshments."

'Jolly good,' Grandpop parked the car neatly. 'Bale out, chaps, and let's re-group in the tea rooms!'

Billy was relieved to get out of the rather cramped seat. And his peckishness had turned to ravenous hunger. They walked through the tearooms to a conservatory at the back.

On the way through, Billy noticed a leather suitcase next to a hat stand. It was covered in stickers from exotic-sounding places and an extraordinarily long name was stamped in black letters on the side: "Featherstonehaugh". He caught a whiff of cigarette smoke and, for some reason, shivered, despite the warmth of the June day. But he was quickly distracted by the cakes on pretty china cake stands in the tea rooms: angel cake and Battenberg cake, fruit cake and Victoria sponge, Madeleines and jam tarts. On top of that there were buns: Chelsea buns, pink-iced buns, teacakes and scones, lardy cake and macaroons. The "Healthy Eating Police" would have thrown their hands up in horror.

As he sat in the conservatory that sunny afternoon, most of a sticky yellow slab of cherry cake and a milky tea with three sugars already "down the hatch", Billy finally had the chance to ask Grandpop a few questions. Questions that had been humming around his head like bees around lavender.

'Grandpop...where are we exactly?'

'Do you mean "where" or "when"?' Grandpop seemed distracted and not over keen to get into conversation.

'Well, both, I suppose. I think...I've gone back in time, haven't I?'

'It would seem so, yes. This is my time, here. I'm certainly not dead or anything preposterous like that. If you really must know, go and have a look at that paper – what's the date on it?'

Billy reached over for the *Daily Express* from the next table:

'20th June 1962.'

'Yes,' said Grandpop, somewhat curtly. '20th June 1962. And I have a briefing at Bigglesbrook at seventeen hundred hours regarding a forthcoming mission to Burmeon, which you'll just have to tag along to.' Billy sensed that Grandpop's annoyance at his presence had resurfaced.

'But, Grandpop...what about Gran? It's quarter to three... she'll be back from the church soon. She'll be worried if I've just disappeared...' The cake and the tea had jogged Billy's memory of where he was supposed to be. While 1962 seemed perfectly comfortable, he didn't really want to cause Gran any unnecessary bother. There might even be a limit to Gran's cool and calm serenity if he just vanished into the thin air of the past.

Grandpop took his pipe out of his mouth, somewhat exasperated. 'Now look here, old chap. The person you call Gran isn't a gran yet, not by a long stretch of the imagination. In fact, she isn't even a mother just yet. If I know her, she's probably pottering around in the garden and maybe putting her feet up under the apple tree to listen to the wireless. I'm certainly no boffin but it seems logical that if you've landed in my time here that time isn't rolling on where you come from simply because it doesn't exist yet. I have said that I'll get you back somehow and I will. In the meantime you'll have to stick with me. It's not going to be exactly easy, having a young nipper slightly surplus to requirements in tow but we'll just have to carry on regardless. Roger?'

'Roger!' Billy smiled. Grandpop was once more in a receptive mood. 'What's this mission all about, then?'

'It's all a bit hush-hush.' Grandpop cocked his head close to Billy's conspiratorially. 'Better wait till we get to Bigglesbrook for the full briefing. Careless talk costs lives and all that.'

38

'And Bigglesbrook is…?' Billy wanted at least one real answer.

Before Grandpop could reply, Monty pricked up his ears, growled and would have bolted through the tearooms and outside had Billy not been quick enough to grab his collar. Grandpop stood up with a quizzical expression on his face:

'Strange…what's eating you, Monty, old boy? It's almost as if something…or some*one*…look here, old chap, we'd better get cracking. You'd best get outside with Monty and I'll settle up here.'

Billy was almost dragged out by Monty, who was still growling. When they got outside, Billy noticed some tracks in the gravel. A whiff of burning rubber and oil hung in the air as if a car had just departed at speed. He looked down the road but there was nothing to be seen. Grandpop marched out of the Lupin Tea Rooms, pipe in mouth and jangling his keys. Monty jumped into the little green car and Billy was just about to follow suit when he noticed something. A cigarette end lay on the ground by the car, still smoking, with a distinctive, unpleasant odour that he knew from somewhere. A picture of that leather suitcase with the stickers leapt into his head. It hadn't been there on his way out, had it?

'Grandpop! Don't start the car up. I've got a funny feeling…don't ask me why, but I think someone could have done something…while we were in there!'

Grandpop looked at Billy. His expression was questioning, serious. He drew on his pipe.

'Hmm…excuse me,' he waved at a motor mechanic on the garage forecourt. 'Old girl here's been playing up a bit. I wonder if you'd look her over…'

The mechanic came over, looked under the bonnet then jacked the car up and looked underneath:

'Your brakes, guv'nor. Just as well you asked me to have a look…I can put it right straight away if you like…'

'I'd be much obliged,' Grandpop slipped him a note and the mechanic went off to fetch his tools.

Once the car was repaired and they were back on the road, Grandpop seemed to forget the rather odd incident of the brakes and, full of tea and cake, Billy tried to put it out of his mind, too. But he sensed a change in Grandpop's acceptance of him and a feeling of pride that he'd been of use instead of "slightly surplus to requirements". And gradually, the warmth and the pleasing sounds of the car and the summer afternoon reassured him and he relaxed – as much as someone who's suddenly landed back fifty years in time can. He shut his eyes, leaned back in the leather seat, faced up to the glorious sunshine and gently stroked Monty's woolly head. He felt a delicious sense of adventure, of being part of something out of a film or a comic. He could do anything in the world.

'Where or what is Bigglesbrook, Grandpop?'

'HQ. In Blighty at least. *And* the scene of the Bigglesbrook International Air Fair next month – something of a first and last. First time we've put on such a show and my last chance to lead the formation flying before I hand over to a younger chap. We'll be there in a jiffy.'

The Austin Healey meandered further along lanes lined with hedgerows and through sleepy towns with duck ponds. As they left one town, Billy felt the car slow down. They'd got stuck behind a tractor. Grandpop grunted a little but remained good-humoured as the tractor puffed and spluttered up a hump-backed bridge.

Hooting, engine revving and cursing behind them shattered the peaceful afternoon atmosphere. Billy glanced in the mirror. The sleek and evil E-Type with its malevolent-looking driver sat right up on the Sprite's tail. Suddenly the car gave an almighty rev. It screeched past Grandpop and the tractor at the brow of the hill. Billy watched, horrified, as a motorcyclist coming from the other direction swerved at the top of the bridge. The man was flung through the air. He landed against the wall of the bridge. The motorbike skidded down the road on its side, leaving the E-Type swooping off regardless into the far distance and the tractor puffing on oblivious.

'Everything all right?' Grandpop leapt out of the Austin Healey and helped the motorcyclist up. Together they looked over the BSA motorbike that had slid and spun around the road but miraculously seemed in one piece.

'Yeah, I reckon so, mister. As long as me bike's OK. My pride and joy, that is…'

'It is a splendid piece of kit,' Grandpop agreed and inspected the bike with the young man. 'You can do without idiots like that fellow, though.'

'I agree, mister. Should never have got his driving test, that one.'

'Sadly, he has his wings, as well,' Grandpop muttered darkly. 'Now, if there's anything we can do for you - drive you to the next garage or whatever, then we'll be more than willing.'

The motorcyclist nodded his thanks but declined the offer, obviously relieved that no major damage was done to his person or his BSA. Billy, Grandpop and Monty climbed back into the car and continued on the journey.

However hard he tried, Billy could not get the image of the E-Type and its devilish driver out of his mind. Had it really been an accident? Billy was sure he had heard a nasty chuckle and seen a triumphant fist waving as the man had sped off. He could see the man's twisted leer on a bony face framed by slick black hair. And... the suitcase at the tearooms with that long name...the particular smell of those cigarettes...that business with the brakes. The penny dropped:

'That accident...it wasn't an accident, was it Grandpop? He meant to do it...that creepy man. And he was at the tearooms. He tried to sabotage your car. He's following us, or after us, or trying to stop us. I saw his suitcase. Some really long name.' He spelled it out. 'F-e-a-t-h-e-r-s-t-o-n-e-h-a-u-g-h. You know who he is, don't you?'

Grandpop sighed. 'I'm afraid so, old chap. Oswald Featherstonehaugh is the wretched fellow's name – yes, you say it as "Fanshaw" – and you can guarantee to get his blood boiling if you get it wrong...a thoroughly bad egg. Still calls himself Squadron Leader although he was drummed out of the RAF years ago. He was caught red-handed stealing a plane. It wasn't the first, either. He had already made a pretty packet "losing" planes, claiming insurance, and then selling the "lost" planes off to all manner of dubious dictators and potty potentates. The sort of crackpots that want to build up their own air force on the path to world domination.'

'Wow.' Billy was stunned. 'So what's he up to now? Why did he fiddle with your brakes and run us off the road?'

'Good question. Bit puzzled myself. Thought old Fanny had done a permanent bunk off to Timbuktu or somewhere – and good riddance. I rather hoped my eyes were playing tricks when I saw him at the wheel of that Jag. But it's pretty clear he's back in Blighty and set on sabotaging our little game here…best be on our guard at all times.' Billy accepted the explanation and tried to keep his curiosity at bay. He sensed that Grandpop was reluctant to talk about Featherstonehaugh any more – but why?

The Austin Healey drove on, through that summer of 1962, past ice cream vans and caterpillar-green woods, across rolling hills, until a sign pointed to RAF Bigglesbrook. The side-road led to a panorama of hangars and runways and prefab huts. And in the middle of it all, like an oasis of elegance and calm, was a splendid white building.

'There we are,' said Grandpop. 'The Officers' Mess, RAF Bigglesbrook. Not quite sure how we're going to play this one, you coming along for the ride and so on, but we'll just have to wing it. Now, first of all, once we're in there, just go along with anything I say. And we'd better stop this "Grandpop" business. I'm Uncle Johnny to you from now on. And…you'd better keep mum about Featherstonehaugh. For the time being, anyway…'

'Grandp…Uncle Johnny, what *is* it with him?' Billy had to know – once they got into the Officers' Mess questions would be impossible. 'There's more to it than you're saying, isn't there? Y'know…I dunno why, but I sometimes get *feelings* about people…and things…and with him…'

'Hmm,' Grandpop glanced at Billy as the Austin Healey nipped up the driveway of the Officers' Mess. An honest, man-to-man look. 'I suppose I didn't want to alarm you unduly but perhaps it's better if you know how the land lies. As I said, Featherstonehaugh was drummed out of the RAF…'

'For stealing a plane, yes…'

'What I didn't say is that I was the one that caught him. Which was a touch tricky, seeing as he was my CO at the time. And since that day…let's put it this way…yes, since that day, you could say he's had it in for me.'

You and me both, now, thought Billy.

Chapter 4

Briefing at Bigglesbrook

'Sixteen hundred thirty.' Grandpop consulted his watch and closed the door of his quarters. He took Monty's lead from Billy. They'd just finished packing the biscuit tin and the rest of the provisions from the Forget-me-not Stores in a khaki travel-bag. 'Not quite over the yardarm but I wouldn't mind a little something. Now, if anyone asks you, not that they will, you're coming over to Burmeon with me as company for the Singh boy. Young Singh. You'll get on like a house on fire. Nothing to do with this mission. You're my nephew, simple as that. To recap, none of this Grandpop stuff. I am Uncle Johnny at all times. A-OK?'

Billy was a bit confused. 'Young Singh...nothing to do with the mission...Uncle Johnny...'

'Got it.' Grandpop nodded. 'Remember – careless talk costs lives.'

Billy was still totally bewildered by everything as they made their way to the big white building but he was driven by an urge to stick to Grandpop, no matter what. Grandpop was the only connection he had to his family and his life before in this weird world of 1962. And Grandpop had promised that he would get Billy back to his own time, somehow.

The inside of the Officers' Mess was as dark and cool as the outside was white and fresh. Wooden floorboards creaked as they stepped into the entrance hall, calm and dignified in contrast to the heat and buzz outside. An impressive staircase swept upwards in a flourish, the walls lined with Air Force crests and paintings of aircraft. Black and white photos of senior officers stared out with looks of resignation at being so important that they were grounded, coupled with a yearning to be back up there, simply flying.

Billy and Grandpop made their way to the bar, a chaotic-looking place compared to the dignity of the entrance hall and staircase. There were enormous leather sofas and armchairs that could double as a small ship. Everything was rather worn and had obviously seen better days. Huge newspapers were strewn around all over the place and one corner looked as if it had been used for an impromptu rugby match.

'Is that why it's called the Officers' Mess? Because it *is* a mess?' Billy's question was genuine.

'Hmm.' Grandpop snorted. 'This, old chap, is spick and span. You should see it when we've got a full house on Battle of Britain day. What will you have? Ginger beer? Mac, old boy, make that a ginger beer for the lad and the usual for me.'

Billy sat at the bar, dangling his legs from the barstool as the barman poured out a ginger beer then mixed a concoction involving a nasty little bottle with dark brown dribbles down the sides for Grandpop. The two men shared a joke and Billy drifted off into a dream, back into the Austin Healey zooming and vrooming around bends in country lanes...

Billy started. The growl of a powerful engine leapt from his daydream onto the gravel forecourt of the Officers' Mess. He knew that sound...

'Grandp...' Billy sat up in panic.

In response, Grandpop went into a major coughing fit with his pipe.

'Come on then – hmph – help your poor old Uncle Johnny out with a pat on the – hmph – back, then!' Grandpop spluttered.

Billy swung around to thump Grandpop between the shoulder blades. Unfortunately this set off a chain of disasters: Grandpop's pipe jumped out of his mouth, leapt across the bar and set a copy of the *Daily Telegraph* on fire, which Mac the barman tried to put out with the remains of Billy's ginger beer.

Billy managed to slap Grandpop's back with one hand but the other collided with the nasty little bottle of dark brown stuff, which spun itself around and threw up all over Mac's starched white shirt. Billy, unbalanced by the whole show, toppled off the barstool and landed on top of a protesting Monty.

Amid the stink of burning *Daily Telegraph*, Angostura bitters, caramelised ginger beer and the howling of disgruntled boy, dog and barman, Grandpop surveyed the aftermath coolly and pronounced, in a carry-on-regardless sort of way: 'Briefing on Burmeon imminent at seventeen hundred. Look sharp, old chap. Room 307.'

Pushing Billy and Monty forward, Grandpop winked at Mac, slipped him a note of indeterminate value and shuffled his charges out of the bar.

On the staircase, Grandpop wiped his brow. 'I'm not 100% convinced that having you tagging along to Burmeon is the brightest of ideas after that little incident, but you do seem to have your uses... now, off we go. I'll be doing the briefing. You'll stay mum unless absolutely necessary. Remember. Young Singh. And I'm your Uncle Johnny.'

In Room 307, a few young officers were gathered. The blinds were drawn and an old projector sat at the end of the table.

'Good afternoon, gentlemen,' Grandpop announced. 'For those that don't know me, I am Squadron Leader Walker, the commanding officer for your forthcoming mission in Burmeon. The young man at the back of the room is Billy, a young relative of mine. I will be flying out to Burmeon with Billy tomorrow in a commercial aircraft for security reasons. You will be following on in a couple of days as per your Joining Instructions. We should easily have the whole thing in the bag in time for the Air Fair – as I'm leading the Hunter formation that day I'm certainly not going to let a spot of bother in the jungle detain me unnecessarily.' The young men laughed and Grandpop continued. 'Now, I have considerable knowledge of Burmeon – the terrain, the flying conditions and importantly, the political background, which I'll be briefing you on today. I will endeavour to keep it short. Kindly keep all questions to the end...lights out, please, Billy.'

Billy fumbled around for the light switch and the old projector whirred into action. Grandpop clunked through a few slides: maps of the country, a grainy photo of a few bungalows surrounded by palm trees – HQ, RAF Botawaddy – various aircraft and helicopters including a lone Sunderland flying boat "in retirement" moored in a lagoon and aerial shots of jungle and sea. Grandpop commented on all this in a serious tone and clicked a swagger stick against the screen to point out items of particular relevance.

Billy wasn't sure whether it was the seriousness of Grandpop's manner, the totally low-tech nature of the clunking slide projector or the idea of that stinky brown stuff all over Mac's shirt but all of this, combined with a feeling that he hadn't slept for days, was making him very light-headed, silly and giggly. He tried to focus on what Grandpop was saying but none of it made much sense. His attention drifted to the window where a shaft of sunlight seemed to be creeping into the darkened room through a crack in the blind. A low buzzing sound accompanied the sunlight in its foray into the room. There was something odd about this – but then again, wasn't it all odd? Going back in time and everything? Billy couldn't trust his normally good sense of perception any more. There were different rules here…

'Now, Burmeon itself is pretty stable, politically speaking, but I must warn you that Botawaddy is only ten miles or so from the border of one of the most inhospitable hotbeds of insurgency in the world today. I am talking, gentlemen, about Ybur.' Grandpop paused to take a sip of water.

'Ybur is small in terms of land area but vast in terms of its economic and political significance. It is a country dominated by jungle, once inhabited only by the legendary mud men of Ybur' – here Grandpop showed a slide of natives caked in whitish mud – 'pygmies, who are reported to be fearless headhunters. Ybur's wealth of rubies and other precious stones was discovered in the last century as Ybur became a Princely State under the British Empire...' Billy's head was beginning to spin with all this information. What on earth was a Princely State? Grandpop's voice carried on. Everything made less and less sense:

'...When independence came to Burmeon after the War, the current ruler, the Wali of Ybur, refused to accede to the Dominion of Burmeon, and the state of Ybur remains independent to this day. Now, this would be no major cause for concern, in the normal course of events. The Wali of Ybur is a harmless enough character when left to his own devices. However, over the last five years, the Wali has increasingly become more of a puppet ruler with the real power in the hands of this man...'

Grandpop clunked momentarily onto a blank slide for dramatic effect:

'Gentlemen: The self-styled General Kwok of Ybur!'

Billy looked up at the larger-than-life character who now loomed on the screen: a huge man in a theatrical gold and white uniform struck a military pose, a jewel-encrusted sabre at his side. The man had a crazed grin, teeth bared, and set into one of them was a ruby, which glistened like a drop of fresh blood.

'Kwok,' continued Grandpop 'trained in the British Army and was, by all accounts, an athletic and brave officer. He saw service in the War in the Far East but unfortunately sustained terrible injuries, which have resulted in an addiction to morphine and other pain-killing drugs. Tragically, the drugs have addled his brain and ridded Kwok of his humanity. Corrupt, cruel and vain, Kwok re-surfaced about ten years ago in Ybur, where his presence has been felt increasingly in acts of aggression within Ybur...'

Billy could take it no more. He had that dreadful feeling that you do sometimes at school when there's something awfully serious being spoken about and all you want to do is crack up. Princely States, tyrannical Generals, the British Empire, puppet rulers and the serious way that Grandpop was conducting the briefing all muddled up in his mind and he desperately wanted to laugh. He closed his eyes, bit on his tongue and tried to think about Call-me-Les or something else equally unfunny.

'... And our latest intelligence suggests that Kwok has recently really overstepped the mark...I will save the exact details of our forthcoming mission for the final briefing at Botawaddy but I am sure, gentlemen, that you can guess its nature...'

As the next slide clunked down and Grandpop tapped the screen with his swagger stick, Billy's laugh exploded through his sealed lips. In desperation, he tried to find an intelligent remark or a searching question to disguise his outburst:

'Is General Kwok a dubious dictator or a potty potentate, Grandpunclejohnny?' he blurted out.

'A crackpot in any case. And you are in danger of becoming a noxious nipper if we have any more of that. Excuse me, gentlemen, but the boy *has* had a rather long journey to Bigglesbrook today. In some ways, it took him ages to get here.' Grandpop glared at Billy, then approached him with a rather fierce look on his face. Billy's giggles died away. 'Look here, old chap. Go and get some fresh air with Monty if you can't cope with any more of General Kwok and his exploits. I can't say I blame you.'

Billy was relieved to leave the darkened room and escape out into the late afternoon sunshine with a similarly relieved Monty. He sat down on the steps leading into the Officers' Mess and looked up at the sky. A lone Chipmunk was circling around: obviously a flying lesson. Uncle Singh, young Johnny, Oswald Featherstonehaugh pronounced Fanshaw, potty potentates, Burmeon, headhunters and Peek Frean's biscuits. This was all going to take some getting used to. Billy took several deep breaths and looked up at the plane dancing in the blue sky above.

But what was that? Something else up there was moving. Not in the sky, but on the roof. It was near to an open window where the blinds were drawn. That must be Room 307, where the briefing was still taking place! Billy stood up, screwed up his eyes and looked at the window. There was a definite gap in the blind – which must have been where the sun was coming in as he'd been sitting there. And there was… something like a microphone attached to a length of cable! It was being drawn away from the window as if by an invisible hand. Could that have had something to do with that buzzing he'd heard? He followed the microphone – or whatever it was – with his eyes, then ran around the side of the Mess and looked up at the roof. Nothing. He turned round. A pilot in flying overalls was walking briskly away from the Mess to the hangars. The man was jagged and angular in his appearance and gait but already too far away for Billy to see him properly. Billy shrugged his shoulders and returned to the steps. Probably his imagination playing tricks.

'Hard work isn't it, chaps. This mission business.' Grandpop had emerged from the Officers' Mess. He gave Monty an energetic handshake and ruffled Billy's hair.

'You can say that again, Grandpop. Uncle Johnny. And what now?' Grandpop's presence gave Billy a reassuring feeling of the real, the here-and-now and dispersed his wild imaginings into the late afternoon sunshine.

'Well, we'll turn in before too long. We'll leave Monty with Mac for the duration: don't want to take him out to Burmeon or – heaven forbid – Ybur. They probably eat dogs out there. Tomorrow we get cracking bright and early. We've got a twenty-three-and-a-half-hour flight ahead of us. First leg is Bigglesbrook-Malta. DC3. Then a bit of luxury on a 707. BOAC. Malta-Bombay. Quick change to a Beverley then off to RAF Botawaddy.' Grandpop's relaxed, in-control manner was infectious. If Featherstonehaugh really were such a threat, Grandpop wouldn't be so cool about everything, would he?

The next day and a half whirled by like the crazy muddle of a dream. From the early morning dew of Bigglesbrook airfield and the loud buzz of the DC3's propellers to the Mediterranean heat of rocky Malta and the glamour and sophistication of the BOAC flight to Bombay. Over a pink gin or two (he was in civvies, after all), Grandpop kept Billy entertained with tales of low level night flying over Burmeon and of an emergency landing prompted by the discovery of a still-sleeping jaguar in one of the engines.

When it got dark outside, Billy was invited to the cockpit. It was amazing how many dials and levers there were. And paper maps and pilots that really flew. The only other time he'd seen a cockpit was a quick glimpse after a charter flight to Greece. It had been all digital and autopilot. On his way back to his seat, Billy caught a whiff of a particularly nasty-smelling cigarette and started to splutter. He looked up and saw the glowing end of the cigarette. It was held in a pair of thin, mean lips under a waxed moustache. Billy saw the eyes of Oswald Featherstonehaugh glare straight at him through the darkness and cloud of evil-smelling smoke. He gulped in astonishment and fear. A nasty twisted smirk passed over Featherstonehaugh's face. Then he turned slowly away to gaze out of the window into the Indian night sky.

Billy shook his head and rushed back to Grandpop, but Grandpop had fallen asleep, head on shoulder, grunting slightly.

When they touched down at Bombay to change onto the much smaller and rough-and-ready Beverley, there was no sign of Featherstonehaugh. Billy seriously began to wonder if he had imagined his presence.

Chapter 5

Radar

The Beverley landed at RAF Botawaddy, Burmeon at mid-day. Its cargo of Billy, his rucksack, Grandpop, Grandpop's battered leather suitcase with its own impressive collection of travel stickers as well as several bags and crates of important supplies were carefully disembarked onto the baking tarmac. Billy felt dizzy as he was hit head-on by the sweltering heat. He gazed up at the sky: deep blue, framed with palm-trees and swelling with threatening clouds.

'Best thing to do is get indoors and get some kip, old chap,' Grandpop looked remarkably composed in a linen suit and Panama hat. 'We've arrived slap-bang at the beginning of the monsoon season. Any moment now it'll bucket it down. That's our quarters, over there.' He indicated a small group of white huts with his pipe. From a flagpole hung an RAF flag. It, too, seemed exhausted in the still, torrid air.

When Billy awoke some hours later, he looked straight up into a mosquito net suspended over the bed like a giant birdcage. Above it, a ceiling ventilator circled and groaned, worn out from the sweltering heat. Outside, the heavy rain pounded incessantly.

Billy stretched his arms above his head and then in a semi-circle to his sides. He turned slightly. He was not alone in the little room. A boy was sitting on the floor, his back against the wall and his long brown legs carelessly crossed in front of him. The boy was eyeing Billy with a curious smile.

'I say. You've been asleep an awfully long time.' The boy's voice was totally incongruous with his appearance. He was a couple of years older than Billy, tall and athletic, his skin tanned a deep woody brown with more than enough signs of scrapes and adventures on his bare arms and legs. He certainly didn't look as if he spent his whole time cooped up in the snooty private school that his accent implied.

'My name's Singh but everyone calls me Radar. My Pater's a Flight Sergeant – the engineer on your Uncle's flight. Officially speaking of course. Unofficially, everyone knows that the two of them run this place,' Radar leaned forward towards Billy as if he thought someone might be listening in who shouldn't be. 'Your Uncle – Squadron Leader Walker – is the most fearless and accomplished pilot this squadron, or perhaps the whole RAF, has ever known. And my Pa – is terrifyingly intelligent. He's got sixth sense. I could tell you stories about stuff the two of them have got up to that would make your hair stand on end...'

Just then, Radar seemed to sense something. His unblinking brown eyes glanced to one side. He moved back against the wall and continued on a completely different tack as if nothing had happened:

'I'm just spending the last couple of weeks of my hols here, actually – shall I call you Billy or Blake? Billy? It really will be ace stuff, having you around. I say, your Uncle asked me if you can borrow some of my clothes so here you are: don't suppose they do tropical kit in England, do they? Oh, speak of the devil; here he is...Squadron Leader Walker!' Radar rose to his feet and stretched out a hand to Grandpop who had just marched into the room, looking ready for action in his tropical kit.

'Young Singh the Radar! I see that you've made the acquaintance of my nephew. Jolly good. Now that I've got to go and report for duty, I wonder if you'd be so good as to give Billy a quick brief on our little – er – spot of bother. With the cat. He might have a bright idea or two. Well – over and out!' Grandpop turned on his heel and strode out of the room like a clockwork soldier.

Radar shrugged his shoulders. 'Oh well, orders are orders. Actually, it'll be terribly exciting if you can help me out...you see... I've got a sort of mission of my own. But...better go somewhere a bit more out-of-the-way. You never know who's listening...'

'Careless talk costs lives and all that,' muttered Billy, still a little sleepy and wondering what on earth he was going to be briefed on next.

Radar laughed, stood up and offered a hand to Billy to drag him out of the bed. 'I think you've got the measure of your uncle and RAF Botawaddy alright!' Billy smiled a lopsided smile back and knew from that moment on that the older boy and he would be the best of mates.

'You can set your watch by the monsoon in Botawaddy,' Radar remarked as they ambled out of the bungalow into the soaked but sunny late afternoon. 'Rain always stops at five-thirty sharp.'

'Totally weird!' Billy's eyes were all over the compound. The glimpse of distant runways, the palms weighed down with tropical rain, the efficient khaki figures strutting in and out of buildings and the flags stretched out sunning themselves after their soaking.

'Why do they call you Radar, then?'

Radar laughed. 'When I was little, my Pa said I picked up on everything and they started calling me Radar-Rajah. When I got to school, there were four Singhs so the Radar bit stuck. And it seems to fit in with the RAF all right where everybody has to have a nickname. Take your uncle, for instance...'

'You mean he's not really called Johnny?'

''Course not! Johnnie Walker's a whisky. They drink gallons of it in the Mess. But not when they're flying, of course...if you want to wind your uncle up, you should try and find out his real name...I bet it's something awful like Percival...or Peregrine...'

'...or Basil!' Billy joined in.

'...or Cuthbert!'

'We'll do the briefing from on high...' They'd reached a group of trees and Radar indicated a makeshift tree house about ten metres up a tree that looked like a monkey-puzzle. 'If they notice us at all, it'll just be a case of – oh, boys will be boys and no questions asked – don't want to attract unnecessary comment. How are you up a tree?'

Billy muttered something about his tree house at home. But he felt quite uneasy about the sheer height of the precarious-looking structure.

'Do what I do and you can't go far wrong!' Radar was already scaling the tree with the elegance of a cat. 'And watch out – it's all rather slippy after that tip-down!'

What Radar had managed in a long-legged, practised matter of seconds took Billy a few minutes, a few false starts, a few slips and one near-disaster. But he made it, with encouragement from Radar. Then the two of them sat like crown princes in the tree, surveying the kingdom of RAF Botawaddy and beyond.

'You're not going to believe what they want us to do!' Radar commenced.

'Go on – hit me with it.' Nothing was going to surprise Billy now.

'Right.' Radar hung his legs in a careless sort of way over the rickety plank they were seated on. Billy had his legs folded up under him and sat slightly nervously, holding onto the tree trunk.

'Over there,' Radar turned and pointed into the distance, 'about ten miles or so, Burmeon ends. Beyond that, is...'

'Ybur,' Billy butted in. 'I know that!'

'Fair enough. But do you know about this ruddy idiot...'

'Kwok. Course.' Billy nonchalantly let one of his legs swing a little over the plank of the tree house.

'Well, naturally, everyone knows about this maniac Kwok. Everyone knows that Kwok is completely driven by greed and doesn't care who he kills or what he destroys to get his hands on more of Ybur's rubies. Everyone knows he wants the rubies to buy guns because he's not going to be content with such a piffling little place as Ybur. Everyone knows he's probably going to wipe out the poor old Wali in some "accident" or another. He really is crazed to high heaven, they say, but what hardly anyone knows about is...' Radar looked around although it was hardly likely that a grown airman had scaled the slippery tree while they weren't watching '...the self-styled General Kwok's plans to decorate his throne-room at the Palace on the Lake.'

'So what's the big deal?' Billy couldn't really imagine why the entire Royal Air Force in this part of the world should give two hoots about whether General Kwok had a diamond chandelier, gold-flocked wallpaper or a Call-me-Les-style jacuzzi.

'Well, of course it's only a big deal if you really know what's been going on, like I do.' Radar paused and sighed.

'After all, I was there. I was the one who saw Kwok's men capture her.'

'*Who* did they capture?' Billy drew his legs back up onto the plank, excitedly.

'Durga,' answered Radar, enjoying Billy's lack of comprehension for a moment or two before continuing. 'Durga is a tigress, one of the last of a very rare sub-species that lives in the jungle on the border of Burmeon and Ybur. I sometimes go to watch them…which is of course very dangerous for the inexperienced…and a couple of days ago, Kwok's men came and captured Durga. She was taken off-guard while feeding her young – she has two cubs. They got her with a tranquilliser dart and bundled her into a cage and took her off to Kwok's Palace on the Lake in Ybur to await her fate…'

'Which is?' Billy could hardly bear to hear but knew he must.

Radar paused. He looked up to the heavens, sighed, and looked at Billy: 'General Kwok wants a tiger-skin rug.'

'Errrh! With a head and everything?'

'With a head and everything. Durga's skin. Durga's head. With two defenceless cubs left in the jungle.' Radar stared across RAF Botawaddy into the mid-distance, direction Ybur.

'What a sicko! But how do you know he hasn't already...you know...that it isn't too late?'

'Neither Kwok nor any of his countrymen can kill Durga. They believe – quite rightly, if you're asking me – that anyone who harms her will be struck down with the most abominable curse ever known to man...for all his arrogance and his British military training, Kwok is still superstitious as hell. He's actually terrified of the Ybur mud men, too, which is why he wants them bombed. And as for Durga, the curse is a pretty good deterrent...'

'So she'll be OK? If they all really believe that. Unless...'

'Unless, Billy, Kwok gets someone else to kill her. Someone who doesn't believe in the curse. A foreigner, maybe an Englishman. Someone with no morals, no belief, no conscience...'

A terrible thought shot into Billy's head. 'Oh, cripes! Oswald Featherstonehaugh. He was with us on the plane. He'd do it, I know...'

Radar stared, resigned, towards Ybur. He grabbed Billy's forearms. 'It's all coming together now. There are plans afoot for the RAF to take Kwok out. I mean bomb the Palace on the Lake. The old Wali has *his* palace in the capital of Ybur so he wouldn't be harmed. But I told my Pa and your Uncle Johnny about Durga and how she's being held in Kwok's palace. They agreed – all off the record of course – that we have to rescue Durga before the RAF go in or before that monster Kwok has her killed. I tried it on my own: there's a tunnel there that I'm just a bit big for but...' He paused and looked at Billy, rather swamped in his borrowed clothes. 'Bingo! That must be what your Uncle had in mind. We have to go in together to rescue Durga before the worst happens...'

'Wow!' Both boys were silent for a few moments as they took in the importance and danger of their mission. The villains' intentions were falling into place like pieces of some diabolical game plan. Killing Durga could be the start of a collaboration that was somewhere beyond evil...

Billy's thoughts were interrupted. He spotted Grandpop and an older man striding across the wet paving stones of the compound. They stopped to exchange a few words, and then marched on towards the monkey-puzzle tree.

'That's the CO – Commanding Officer,' Radar whispered to Billy. 'Let's try and hear what they're rabbiting on about. It probably concerns us!'

Billy and Radar lowered their heads a little and kept perfectly still in the post-monsoon sunshine. They could hear

68

snatches of conversation between the two men: Grandpop's voice excited, insistent and the CO's more deliberate and unsure.

'...It's certainly somewhat irregular...not just civilians but children for God's sake...'

'...I will take full responsibility as the boy's guardian, sir. You must believe me, it's our last and only chance without using undue force. And you know my feelings on *that*, sir, unless you wish me to repeat them...'

'...I suppose I will have to trust your judgement, Walker. But please think it through once more...if there really isn't an alternative strategy...young Singh is one thing...but a little English fellow who's still wet behind the ears and doesn't know the first thing about the way of the jungle...'

'...Believe me, sir. Young Billy has capabilities and tricks up his sleeve that even he doesn't know about. He's from...'

Grandpop looked from side to side and moved close to the CO's ear. Billy couldn't hear what passed between them. But the CO raised his eyebrows. Grandpop nodded. The CO patted him on the back, and then walked away towards the palm trees, shaking his head in disbelief but smiling the while.

A little later, over supper in the Mess, Billy was introduced to Radar's "Pater", Flt Sgt Singh, an intense and initially alarming man with slightly mad eyes. But Billy quickly warmed to "Flight" as he told tall story after tall story about the jungle and its natural and rather unnatural history, about which he knew everything. He was the sort of man who, if you happened to want to know whether the *Diplodocus* or the *Brontosaurus* ate more plant material per hour, would not only tell you to the nearest gram, but would also tell you the average circumference of the resulting droppings for good measure.

Over a delicious meal of curried chicken, they were briefed on the mission to rescue Durga.

Kwok's palace was on an island in a lake. Grandpop was to fly the boys to the edge of the lake from where they'd row a boat to the island then enter Kwok's palace via a tunnel from a disused ruby mine, already located by Radar and his father. The Singhs had reached a point at which they could progress no further, as the tunnel became very narrow, too narrow even for Radar to climb through. But they had calculated, through a complicated method involving echoes and throwing pebbles, that this impasse was not very long and led to a large chamber underneath the palace. From this chamber, they had heard the voice of a tigress pining for her cubs: Durga.

When Billy told the two RAF men about his sighting of Featherstonehaugh on the flight and his suspicion about the bugging of the meeting at Bigglesbrook, everybody agreed that there was no time to be lost. The combination of the power-crazed Kwok and the mercenary Featherstonehaugh could lead to anything – even full-scale war. They would go in first thing the next morning.

Billy and Radar were about leave to turn in for the night when the Mess door was flung open. A young aircraftman burst in from the dark tropical night in a state of agitation. Controlling himself, he stood to attention but stammered as he addressed his seniors:

'Squadron Leader Walker, Sir! Flt Sgt Singh, Sir! I have something to report, Sir!'

'At ease, Aldersmith. Now, what is it?'

'One of our aircraft is missing, Sir. The Sunderland: she's gone!'

'Good God!'

'How the devil...?' Grandpop and Flt Sgt Singh looked at each other, obviously came to the same conclusion and rushed out of the Mess. Together with the airman, they ran in the direction of the lagoon where the Sunderland had been moored.

Chapter 6

The palace on the lake

'Come on, bung this lot in your knapsack!' Radar passed an assortment of items to a still-sleepy Billy. Billy found himself stuffing lengths of string, a knife, a torch, candles, matches and a few of the Peek Frean's biscuits into his rucksack. His hands were on automatic pilot but his thoughts were all over the place. There was the missing plane, for a start. He'd learned from Radar that the Sunderland flying boat was actually the last of what had been a whole fleet at RAF Botawaddy and was now "in retirement", moored in a lagoon some way off from the main compound. It was pretty obvious who had been responsible for the theft but the mystery now was: what could Featherstonehaugh's motives be? Where had he taken the flying boat? And then there was the "special mission". And here was Billy, at some unearthly hour, halfway across the world and half a century back in time setting off to rescue a tiger from an unbelievably cruel fate. Even *Ajay's Adventures* had nothing on this!

In the freshness of the tropical dawn, they met Grandpop on the runway, standing proudly in his flying suit by a very smart-looking plane.

'Hawker Hunter,' Grandpop patted the plane. 'An absolutely magnificent piece of kit. Recco, fighter, bomber, transport. Does the lot. Supremely manoeuvrable and a joy to fly – roll on the Air Fair, and leading the formation! However, we won't be taking the Hunter this time. Far too conspicuous and not so easy to land in the middle of the jungle. We'll need to take that unassuming little chap over there. De Havilland Chipmunk. Learned to fly in one of those. Just the ticket for what we have to do.' Grandpop led Billy and Radar over to the little training plane and swung himself up into the pilot's seat. 'Right! Let's get cracking and get this kite off the ground!'

Billy climbed on board and squeezed next to Radar on the tandem seat of the Chipmunk. Ahead of them, Grandpop checked the controls.

Driving with Grandpop in the Austin Healey Sprite had been an amazing experience. But it was dull as ditchwater in comparison to the Chipmunk. The tiny size and basic-looking controls on the plane just added to the excitement. Billy had been on plenty of fairground and theme park rides but none of them came close to this. On those, you just went on a set course but flying with Grandpop had infinite possibilities. There was the amazing noise and vibration at take-off. And that feeling of your stomach gulping as the plane left the runway. And then the glorious feeling of soaring and swooping across the skies as if you owned them. Billy grinned at Radar and looked up through the cockpit bubble at the endless blue Asian skies. Almost involuntarily, he felt himself banking and leaning with the aircraft as it turned and glided. As he looked down, he saw that his hands were grasping imaginary controls.

Far too soon for Billy's liking, they landed on a scruffy strip of concrete in the middle of some dry bush land. To the left of the strip was more open country, all dried grass and a few prickly-looking stumpy trees. On the right, the terrain appeared to get swampy and densely packed with bamboo and mangrove.

'We're almost on the border of Ybur,' Grandpop glanced eastwards. 'I won't come with you this time. Radar, you know the drill. Through the swamp to the lake. Into the boat and over to the island. You know how to find the entrance to the underground passage. Now, old chap,' he turned to Billy, who was fumbling in his rucksack. 'You are the scout this time. Young Singh here is your security, your cover. But it's strictly recco only: no heroics, no funny stuff. Find out where and how the – uh - hostage is being held and report back. I'll hang on here, keep an eye on the plane, and be ready to pick you up at 13:00. If you're not back by then I'll have to take emergency measures and go in myself. Or call reinforcements. But it won't come to that. Synchronise watches?'

Billy and Radar set their watches and waved goodbye to Grandpop. They set off over the landing strip towards the clumps of dried grass and bamboo. Billy felt a little unnerved that his watch from the next century still functioned. Even more unnerving was the fumble in his rucksack. This had resulted in a collision with the inevitable matches, bits of string and other necessities for the mission but also with the undeniable compact modernity of his mum's camera, which he'd as good as forgotten.

But there was no time now to ponder time-travel and the consequences of carrying 21st century technology around in the 20th century world. Radar was bigger, older and infinitely more experienced than Billy in jungle missions. He'd already leapt several grass islets ahead.

'Billy – we haven't the whole day, you know!' Billy sprung to the next clump of grass and put his 21st century mind on idle. By the time they reached the edge of a lake, he was quite getting the hang of it all. He leapt now just as confidently as Radar.

Bamboos surrounded the edge of the lake. Radar brushed a large clump of them aside to reveal a small canvas inflatable boat with a couple of paddles.

'Good. Just as we left it last time. Righty-ho! It's off to the island.'

Billy was sceptical. 'But isn't it all a bit dangerous? What if the potty potentate or dotty dictator or whatever he is – General Kwok, I mean – or his men see us. They'll shoot us on the spot, won't they?'

Radar sighed. 'Billy, can you see the island?'

Billy looked. 'Um...no...not really.'

'Then there's no danger they can see you. The lake curves round where we are, and even when we get within visibility of the island – theoretically speaking, at least – there's a sort of backwater hidden behind a row of mangrove trees. We approach this way, right to the back of the palace, which is built on a huge outcrop of rock anyway – the tradesmen's entrance, if you like. It's all thick with vegetation so you can always just duck down until danger has passed. And...believe me; we're far too interesting for them to shoot us outright. Especially you. They'd capture us first and try to get us to talk. And at that point your Uncle Johnny would be bound to come rushing in like the 7th cavalry...'

'Well OK, then, if you say so...but are there like piranhas or something in that swamp or lake or whatever you call it?'

Radar sighed again. 'I'm not sure what sort of poppycock they teach you wherever you go to school but anyone with even the most basic education in simple biology should know that this type of habitat would not support *Pygocentrus* for five minutes. *Pygocentrus* is only found in South America.'

'We don't get around to anything interesting like that with all the tests and stuff they have to cram in. If we're really lucky, we get a project on Saving the Planet.'

Radar smiled, his dark eyes filling with sympathy. 'But how dull. And how absurd. And how arrogant! This planet doesn't need saving – in the 4 billion years it's been around it's been in worse scrapes than whatever one silly little species can inflict on it. What they mean, Billy, is not saving the planet, but saving themselves. It's all balderdash and piffle. Come on – let's get cracking on our mission to save Durga instead!'

Radar seemed relieved that Billy didn't make any further enquiries about the fauna of Ybur's lakes.

They climbed into the boat and pushed off. The sun was warming up as they paddled through the swampy edges of the lake, through little backwaters and in between curiously shaped overhanging trees and bushes. They got into a rhythm, paddling and pushing off against any vegetation that met their path.

Billy caught a glimpse every now and again of the middle of the lake and the island rising out of the water where Kwok's palace was situated. But Radar had been right – these were only momentary glimpses and the little boat would quickly get lost amongst the greeny-brown of the plants that shielded it reassuringly from view.

They gradually approached a huge rock, covered with more weird vegetation. In front of it was a small bay with a few rocks and bushes. Radar stopped paddling and leapt out of the boat. He hauled it up and moored it between two of the rocks.

'This is the back of the island. The secret tunnel is just over there. It's part of an old ruby mine. I tried to get through with my Pater a couple of days back when your Uncle Johnny brought us but it seems that the blasted tunnel has filled itself in again over the years and I simply couldn't get through. But you'll make it no probs. I was almost at the end of the tunnel when I got stuck – I could hear Durga as if we were in the same cage. I tried to introduce myself but she wasn't exactly in a welcoming mood.'

Radar led Billy towards the gigantic towering rock. At the side of a large mossy-covered stone with a slim gap beside it, he stopped:

'OK – this is where we go in. We should rope ourselves together like climbers or potholers in case there's any bother. Once you're through the tight spot, I'll tug on the rope if there's any funny business. Right – torch at the ready?'

It was a relief to get away from the sweltering sun into the cool tunnel. Near the entrance, both boys could walk upright, Radar ducking his head just a little. Initially, Billy's eyes were blinded from the glaring sunshine outside but he soon grew accustomed to the dark, indistinct contours and curves of the tunnel in torchlight. Alone, it would have been spooky beyond belief. But Radar's reassuring presence behind him gave Billy courage as he walked, then stooped and finally crawled through the serpentine passage deep under Kwok's palace.

At first, the tunnel had been very quiet in contrast to the jabbering of jungle birds and chirping of countless unseen insects outside: Billy just heard the immediate sounds of their breathing and scuffling along the cool floor of the tunnel. Occasionally, he or Radar would scrape a shin against a rock jutting out where it shouldn't or bang a shoulder where the tunnel took an unexpected turn. Then there'd be rude mutterings, followed by much sniggering and "shhh-ing".

After a while, Billy decided that he was better off removing his rucksack and pulling it and himself along, commando-style, than crawling on all fours. It was also clear, from the grunting, muttering and "shhh-ing" that Radar was getting further and further behind. Suddenly, Billy felt a tug on the rope around his waist and Radar's penetrating whisper:

'Stop, Billy! Hold it just there. Now, listen!' Billy rested on his stomach; arms stretched into the dwindling space ahead and listened. A faint but echoing wailing sound came from the tunnel ahead. And then he heard something extraordinary. A similar low cry, totally inhuman, came from behind him. Then silence. Again, the strange cry from behind. And then a roar of fearful intensity shook the whole tunnel. Billy froze. Was he really going to have to go and face *that?*

'Right, Billy – here goes! Durga is there! She should know you're a friend but, well, she's not exactly the pussycat from next door. You need to squeeze through the tunnel here, then it will open up and you'll find her. See how she's being held and where, what sort of cage, what sort of lock. Don't hang around there too long. Don't get too close. You never know. Keep the rope round you. Ready?'

Radar's self-assurance and what seemed like an amazing gift of communicating with tigers gave Billy the guts to press on. Not that he had much choice. But what was it again he had to do? It had been on his mind all day. Yes! His secret from the 21st century that his mother's stress-induced absent-mindedness and a few more twists of fate had landed in some obscure banana republic in 1962. He groped around in his rucksack for the camera and stuffed it into his shorts pocket.

'OK then – I'm going in. I'm leaving my rucksack here – it's too tight for that and me...'

'Good luck then, Billy. Go for it!'

Billy hauled himself, wriggled and rolled through the narrow dark tunnel. He pushed forward with his feet when he felt a foothold. He felt a cool breeze around his head. He whistled quietly and noticed the change in the acoustics. Checking on the rope around his middle and the camera in his pocket, he gave a mighty push with both hands. Yes! This must be it! He had a sudden impression of freedom and space after the confinement of the tunnel.

He was in a chamber. Hesitantly, he rose to kneeling, then crouching, and then standing. He couldn't believe there was room for him, after all this time crawling on his belly. Ahead, around a corner, he saw light. He crept forward slowly, pressed himself against the wall of the chamber and peeked around the corner.

After the darkness of the tunnel it was a shock to be able to see. Billy's gaze turned first upwards, to the source of the light, a couple of tiny windows way above him in the stone wall. His glance slunk downwards, following the daylight that trickled from the windows. Ahead of him were three cells, each bearing a barred door with a substantial lock. At some time this must have been a dungeon. Billy checked the first two cells. Empty. He tiptoed forward and approached the iron door of the third cell. He caught his breath. His eyes met another pair! As green as emeralds, they stared out from a striped feline face. A face he already knew from the kaleidoscope.

'Durga,' whispered Billy and instinctively leapt backwards. The huge cat swung a giant paw towards him. Surely that strength could break the cage? Billy stood transfixed, terrified, like a tiny mouse. But as Durga opened her jaws to roar, a low wailing came from far off. Radar! The tiger sat back on her haunches, still tense, still poised…

The strange sounds coming from deep in the tunnel spurred Billy into action. He took the camera from his pocket and switched it on.

'Just taking some quick pics, Durga. Don't be frightened – we're going to get you out of here,' he whispered. He aimed the camera at the cell, the door, the lock, zooming and snapping.

While snapping hectically, Billy felt a tug on the rope around his middle. And what was that? Footsteps, approaching from beyond the dungeon. He retreated back around the corner.

Billy crouched in the entrance to the tunnel, in semi-darkness and out of view from the cells. He clutched the camera tightly. He didn't dare squeeze back into the tunnel as that would make too much noise. He bit on his lip and tried to keep still. The main door to the dungeon creaked open. He heard two pairs of footsteps, one dull and heavy and the other sharp and metallic on the stone floor. Both stopped by Durga's cage. Billy heard voices:

'Here is the beast, Sir Squadron Leader. I beg you, Sir, not too near, for your safety.'

'Humph! I have no fear of such a creature although I must say this is a damned fine specimen.' The voice was like cold steel. Billy knew exactly whose it was. 'She'll make the General a fine rug: I certainly wouldn't mind such a trophy myself.'

'But Sir Squadron Leader, I do feel it is my duty to remind you once more of the possible consequences of your undoubtedly courageous action – I speak, of course, of ...' the word was whispered, 'the *curse* that shall befall he who slays the most terrible of the beasts of the jungle...'

'Oh for God's sake, man, enough of your mumbo-jumbo and let's think about the practicalities of this...um...execution. We don't want anything too messy as it will spoil the pelt...obviously we need the head intact...I think a knife to the heart will do the trick but we'll need to dope the animal first...how are the General's...er...medication supplies? A couple of days' dosage should be enough to calm the beast down sufficiently...'

The other man muttered something about the General's supplies being critically low and having to make his way to an apothecary in Ybur City, a journey that would take at least 24 hours.

'Even with General Kwok's newly-secured transport?'

'I am afraid, Sir Squadron Leader, that the terrain around Ybur City is such that this would be an impossibility...'

'For God's sake! I despair sometimes about this primitive hole but there'll be no tiger skin without it. I'm damned if I'm going to tackle this monster wide-awake, chained, imprisoned or not. So 24 hours it will have to be and then it's curtains for you, pussycat!'

Billy could only imagine what was happening a few feet away from him. He heard a terrible roar, screams and the sound of the two men toppling on top of each other with much cursing and muttering. The roaring continued. This was the chance that Durga had made for him. Under cover of the racket going on by the cells, Billy dived headfirst back into the narrow tunnel. He squeezed and wriggled his way back to where Radar was waiting.

'Damn and blast that rotten cowardly scoundrel!' Radar hissed. 'It makes my blood boil. I'd have his skin for a rug if it wasn't so white and ugly! I take it that was our friend Featherstonehaugh?'

'Didn't actually see him but I guess so. It felt like him, if you know what I mean.'

'Slimy, sick and yellow-bellied?'

'Yeah, right. But at least we have some time. And I've got a pretty good idea of the cell thing and the lock...'

'A pretty good idea?'

'Call it a photographic memory, if you like.'

Chapter 7

The stolen Sunderland

The heat struck Billy like a slap round the face as he and Radar emerged from the cool darkness of the tunnel. They made their way back to where the boat was tied up. Radar was swinging his arms and whistling, but stopped abruptly just before the boat. He glanced at his watch and turned to Billy with a knowing and slightly mischievous look:

'Are you thinking what I'm thinking about what that rotter Featherstonehaugh referred to as "General Kwok's newly-secured transport?"'

'That it's secured somewhere round here, you mean...?' Billy answered slowly. 'Well, yeah, ...but...don't you think we should get back? Uncle Johnny did say recco only, no heroics...'

'Oh, don't talk rot! It *is* recco...for the missing plane! That would be the real icing on the cake if we find the stolen Sunderland as well as Durga...and now that we're here, all we have to do is jump into the boat and paddle round the side of the island a bit...anyway, we've got bags of time...'

Billy was far from convinced. To be honest, it was a huge relief to have got away from Featherstonehaugh undetected. To risk being spotted from the other side of the palace was pushing their luck a bit. But he looked at Radar and the older boy's spirit of adventure gave him confidence:

'OK then, I suppose...but only if we just sneak a quick look and go back if we don't see anything right away...'

They jumped into the boat and pushed off into the lake, paddling around the side of the island. The sun was blisteringly hot and it was refreshing to have the odd splash of water from the paddles. Billy felt a sense of inevitability as they made their way around the corner to see first the tip of a wing, then an engine, then fuselage, then the whole majestic white bird bobbing gently on the sun-drenched lake. They stopped paddling and gazed ahead at the Sunderland. Radar turned to Billy:

'Are you game for climbing on board and having a quick reccy?'

'Um...don't you think that's a bit risky? I mean, Featherstonehaugh might be on board...'

'Billy, old chap. Use your eyes. The main door is on the left hand side, facing the island. If anyone was on board, they'd have tied a little dinghy up there, unless they flew from the palace! If you're worried, we can tackle it from the right hand side, where there's another door, by the tail plane. That way, we won't be seen at all, even from the palace. Now that we're here...'

'We might as well...' Billy's excitement at climbing around the flying boat was getting the better of his fear. They paddled quickly to the right hand side of the huge white craft and moored their boat by the fuselage. The door required a fair deal of pushing before it opened with a loud squelch. Billy and Radar hoisted themselves inside the cavernous fuselage. It was cool and echoing in here, not unlike the tunnel they'd recently emerged from, but the smell was different – slightly musty mixed with oil and kerosene and an incongruent note of forgotten school dinners.

'Crikey!' whispered Radar. 'I feel like one of those chaps who got swallowed by a whale!'

They walked towards the nose, passing the bomb racks – empty, of course – and the access to the dorsal gun turret above them. The way grew lighter as they approached the front section of the plane where portholes let in the daylight.

'Cool!' gasped Billy. 'There are even bunks in here. And a kitchen. Must be where that horrid stink's coming from!'

'Or from here!' Radar laughed and opened a door behind which was a real porcelain flush toilet. 'Come on, let's get up this ladder – the cockpit must be this way.'

The boys climbed up into the cockpit and spent a good few minutes trying the seats for size, fiddling with the central column, flicking switches to and fro and trying to de-fathom the various dials and instruments. Billy completely lost himself in a dream of climbing from the turquoise lake into the pure blue sky, soaring and swooping over the shimmering waters...

'Oh damn it, Billy. We need to scramble!' Radar's urgent voice brought Billy straight back to earth. He glanced out of the cockpit window.

A motorboat carrying Oswald Featherstonehaugh, General Kwok, huge and resplendent in a scarlet uniform, and a fearsome-looking bodyguard approached the Sunderland from the island.

'Quick – we can't get back now. Too risky. Let's hide in the khazi!' Radar pulled Billy down the ladder and dragged him into the toilet cubicle, locking the door. Billy felt his heart thumping – and Radar's too, so closely were they squeezed together in the uncomfortable little room. He heard the door open. The three men climbed on board; one clearly athletic, with sharp, metallic footsteps, one heavy and deliberate and one amid much cursing and groaning, accompanied by the thump of a heavy walking stick. Billy swallowed and glanced at Radar. Radar's eyes were shut, his nostrils slightly flared as he breathed heavily in and out, his fists clenched. He seemed to be willing something to happen.

Three sets of footsteps passed the boys' hiding place. Billy heard the men making their way down the fuselage, Featherstonehaugh pointing out features of interest to the General:

'...Gun turrets front, dorsal, bow, tail...a truly magnificent old craft, my esteemed General...and she can carry up to 2,000lbs of bombs, mines, depth charges, whatever you like...'

'Whatever we need to bomb those savages to bits! With maximum loss of life!' came a loud booming voice, followed by a deep and malevolent roar of laughter. 'And where are the bombs, exactly, Squadron Leader?'

'Something I'm working on, my dear General. Everything in good time...the mud men will be bombed, the riches of their territory will be yours...I also hope to secure a fighter to complement your air power...but, if you'll forgive me, General, I do have another pressing task to attend to for your Excellency...'

'Ah, yes. My throne room. Good, Squadron Leader. Move on!'

Billy heard the footsteps and the thump of Kwok's stick approaching. His mouth was dry. The thought that the villainous trio were just centimetres away brought him out in a sweat.

'And this area?' General Kwok sniffed and burst into a guffaw. 'Standards of comfort have barely improved since my regrettable time in His Majesty's Forces.'

'Oh,' Featherstonehaugh answered dismissively 'the usual offices – for the crew. Sleeping, eating and other bodily functions. You can always inspect them at your leisure once we've been up on the bridge, as we used to say.'

Billy looked at Radar, who nodded. This might be their chance. They listened as Featherstonehaugh and the bodyguard helped the lumbering and cursing Kwok up the ladder to the upper deck. As they listened, something else was clear. The heat in the cubicle hadn't merely been down to nerves. Outside, the wind was blowing and the first drops of rain had begun to fall. Billy checked his watch. Wasn't it a bit early for the monsoon? He looked at Radar, who rolled his eyes upwards, smiled, and mouthed something with a look of complete triumph across his face.

The boys crept out of the room like cats. Kwok's deep cruel laughter, Featherstonehaugh's monologue on the joys of the Sunderland and his own skill in "securing it" plus the sound of the wind outside gave them enough cover to sneak back along the fuselage. They pushed open the squelchy door and leapt into their waiting boat. Billy grabbed the paddle. He didn't dare look behind him. He focussed on paddling away, through the heavy raindrops that fell like water bombs. It was only when they were well around the corner of the island that he felt the tension ease, and pride at what they'd risked and discovered took over.

The boys were soaked but in good spirits as they made their way back through the mangrove swamps with the boat and then on foot. The downpour had been a short one. The sun streamed down on the wet concrete of the landing strip. Grandpop was waiting for them, leaning nonchalantly against the wing of the Chipmunk.

'Well, chaps?' he grinned. 'Time to regroup and debrief. Chocks away to Botawaddy!'

Back at base, Radar, his father, Billy and Grandpop sat in Grandpop's quarters to report back on stage one of the mission and to plan the next stage. Billy and Radar were both so over-excited and relieved to be back to safety that they were babbling nineteen-to-the-dozen about every detail of their adventure so far: Durga, the medication, Featherstonehaugh and the stolen Sunderland.

'Now, now, steady on, hold your horses,' Grandpop carefully unpeeled a banana as he spoke. 'Let's concentrate on the cat rescue – not that it's strictly speaking what I should be concerned with. I've got that about the tunnel width,' – one flap of banana skin down – 'and Featherstonehaugh's role in all this, damn him' – another flap of banana skin – 'and that we've got at least 24 hours' – he unpeeled the last flap 'but…what we really need to know is: how are we going to de-cage the cat?' He bit into the banana and looked quizzically at the boys. Billy also felt Flt Sgt Singh's eyes fixed intently on him. He *knows* I've got something, Billy thought.

'I've…er…got some photos…close-ups, I mean, of the cage and the lock…on this.' Billy carefully took the camera out of his pocket and held it in front of him. He looked at Grandpop. 'I think *you* know where the camera came from, Uncle Johnny. You'll all have to stand behind me if you want to have a look.'

Without a word, the three of them moved behind him. Billy was relieved he couldn't see Radar and Flt Sgt Singh's initial reactions to 21st century technology. He held the camera in outstretched arms and slowly played through the pictures - Durga, the cell, the door and numerous close-ups of the lock.

'Absolutely amazing...' breathed Flt Sgt Singh. 'Of course, I have dreamed it but never, never did I believe that I'd see it for myself. Young man, if I can borrow this splendid, remarkable piece of technology that you hold in your hands, I promise I can fashion the key to open that lock in the next few hours. Extraordinary what they have in England these days, my son!' Did Billy detect a vague smile cross that normally earnest face?

'I never doubted that we had the right team here. Splendid work, chaps!' Grandpop was evidently more than pleased but he spoke with urgency. 'And I know that Flight will be able to do his stuff sorting out that key. We've already got an incredibly nifty tunnel-blowing device, in a Peek Frean's biscuit tin of all things, thanks to his ingenuity. Now, I suggest that we leave him to do his jiggery-pokery with the key while you young nippers get some rest. I'll report back on the Sunderland to the powers that be, work out some details of ops and see which kite we can use for Stage 2. I'll be over to do a briefing at 18:30. It'll be a short night so you'll need all the rest you can get. But, jolly good show all round!'

Having a rest was hardly easy. Billy was relieved when his watch showed it was nearly half-past six, the hour confirmed by Grandpop's efficient arrival. Grandpop got straight into explaining how Stage 2 was going to run, in theory. To let Durga out of the cage, using the key that Flt Sgt Singh was busy making; both boys would have to get through the tunnel so that Radar could use his tiger-taming and talking skills. They were going to go in as before but take explosives to blast the tunnel at the narrow section just before the dungeon. To this end, Flt Sgt Singh had prepared a bomb in the Peek Frean's biscuit tin which they were to take with them in the boat. The theory was then that they would escape back through the tunnel with Durga and would be hoisted to safety outside by Grandpop and Flt Sgt Singh in a waiting helicopter. It all sounded terrifically exciting but not without danger.

'What if someone hears the explosion in the palace and comes after us?' Billy was still shaken by his mounting number of close brushes with Featherstonehaugh.

'And what if we're too late and they are already down there with Durga when we get through?' Radar's main concern was Durga herself.

'We won't be too late. We're starting before the crack of dawn cracks. And don't worry about the noise. Flight's ingenious devices have a silencer built in.' Grandpop was confident and had an answer for everything.

The crack of dawn had indeed not yet cracked when Billy and Radar were summoned from under their mosquito nets the next morning. Outside, everything was pale green-grey and a heavy mist cloaked the entire compound of RAF Botawaddy.

'We're heading for a real scorcher today, chaps,' remarked Grandpop as they strode towards the hangars and runways. 'Best get as much as we can done before the sun hits the meridian.'

'Now, lads,' Flt Sgt Singh walked on the other side of the boys and spoke in a whisper, the whites of his eyes flashing in an eccentric dance. 'The bomb and the key. The key and the bomb. The bomb is foolproof: just think of it as a handy little mixture of everyday household supplies. Weed killer and sugar. Stinks a bit, like candyfloss. You'll think you're at the jolly old fairground! The fuse is inside the tin and the whole thing is wrapped up in oilskins to keep it dry. It has to be dry. And the key...well, the key is self-evident, too...'

'So, here we are,' Grandpop marched up to a waiting helicopter on the runway. 'We're going to do a bit of the old vertical stuff today. Westland Whirlwind. Just the job for a jungle rescue. All aboard for the completion of Operation Pussycat!'

The tropical dawn chorus became muted as Billy climbed into the Whirlwind. He plopped down onto a squashy leather seat next to Radar. Neither of them spoke. Grandpop and Flt Singh Singh took their seats at the controls. Then all contact with the outside world was shut with the door, the sounds of nature drowned out by the rattle of engines and the whir of the propellers. There was no going back now. Billy felt the helicopter rise up from the earth, moving upwards but not forwards, like being in a huge, noisy Ferris wheel. He turned away from Radar to the Perspex window. It was a slightly eerie experience to see the colour gradually coming to the world around with the dawn. Muted grey-green was replaced with bursts of brilliant blue, rich brown and deep emerald. The key, clutched tightly in his hands, drew his attention away from the outside and back to his friend. Radar held the Peek Frean's tin bomb, wrapped in waxed canvas, grimly in his grip.

Amid the loud whir of the Whirlwind, Billy's nerves started buzzing, too. Here they were with some tin pot bomb, in a creaky and noisy helicopter, about to brave their way through head-hunter mud men and piranhas (whatever Radar said), off to blast open a tunnel...into the palace of some completely mental banana republic would-be dictator. And his side-kick, who probably qualified for being the most evil man on earth. But it didn't stop there. They were going to rescue what could be a man-eating tiger for all he knew. And even if they did succeed up to there – then what? What *was* going to happen when they got Durga out of the cage? She wasn't exactly going to turn round and purr like the cat on the Whiskas ad, was she? Billy shut his eyes and swallowed. There was no going back now…

Once they landed at the concrete strip near the border, Billy had no time to think as Grandpop shot out their orders:

'Right, chaps. You know the drill. Boat – back entrance – bomb – key – big cat rescue – about turn – airlift. Roger?'

'Johnny. Uncle Roger,' Billy's grin was mainly bravado. Radar's eyes rolled in exasperation in a pretty good imitation of his father.

This time, both Radar and Billy leapt over the tufts of grass towards the boat's bamboo-bedecked hidey-hole like young hares, without hesitation. The boat was, reassuringly, as they left it. They took care to stow the biscuit tin in the bottom of the boat where it was least likely to get splashed from the paddling then lost no time in jumping in and pushing off towards Kwok's palace and its prisoner.

Chapter 8

The mud men of Ybur

'I'll tell you what,' Billy puffed as they paddled. 'Either we're paddling with turbo-power this time or Uncle Johnny was right about it being a scorcher!'

'Or both,' replied Radar, taking a break from paddling to sweep his floppy dark hair away from his forehead. 'It really is damned hot.' He peeled off his T-shirt.

'Good move,' Billy took his T-shirt off, too. It was a relief to be rid of that clammy and sticky feeling against his skin.

They made good progress, despite the burning sun, through the little backwaters and between clumps of mangrove trees and overhanging vegetation. Where the lake curved round they caught a glimpse, once more, of the outcrop of rock on the island on which Kwok's palace stood. They had far more of a sense of purpose this time, knowing exactly where they were heading, and why. Their eyes were firmly fixed on the target ahead rather than the surrounding scenery.

'Whaaaa...?' Something flew past from a direction that Billy least expected, the mainland. He caught a glimpse out of the corner of his eye: glistening jewelled colours. A bird or a dragonfly, perhaps? But it had flown too quickly, too directly. And then another, from another direction. He realised, just as Radar yelled out to him:

'Darts! We're under attack! Abandon ship!' Without thinking, his heart beating fast, Billy scrambled out of the boat. As he slithered down into the water, he caught sight of a few small, squat white figures on the far shore of the lake. They were holding blowpipes.

'Oh crumbs and crikey! It's the mud men of Ybur!' Billy joined Radar clinging onto the ropes behind the shield of the boat. 'What are we going to do, Radar?'

Radar looked at Billy, breathing heavily. 'We're going to hang on here…' he ducked a dart '…until…' another one '…they get bored of their little game, run out of darts…' another one '…and go home.'

'Oh, yeah?' Billy was finding the sensation of dangling in seriously muddy and slimy water with (probably) poison darts hurtling across his head most unpleasant. 'And what if they get their bows and arrows going once the darts run out?'

'They don't have them. That's South America,' grimaced Radar, dodging another dart.

'And what's to stop them wading or swimming out here to get us, then? It can't be that deep.'

'Hmm,' Radar flared his nostrils and wrinkled his brow. 'Well, they're pygmies. So they won't be tall enough to wade anywhere.'

'Yeah, right.' Billy wasn't convinced. Peeping round the side of the boat, he was sure that some of the menacing mud men were advancing towards the water.

'Actually, they can't swim. They don't have swim trainers and floats and rubber rings out here for mud men children to learn with.' Radar coughed in a rather unconvincing way.

'Ha, ha – and I'm the crown prince of Ybur! Are you one hundred percent sure they won't try and swim out here?'

'Absolutely. Look, Billy – if you really must know, I expect they fear that there might be crocodiles or something lolling around in here.' Radar's eyes flickered from side to side and he suppressed a giggle.

'Oh, brilliant! I was so worried about the piranhas I forgot about the crocodiles!' Billy was quite tempted to bash Radar one but didn't really want to let go of the boat ropes. They hung on where they were, up to their necks in muddy water. Every now and then, Billy felt something tickle around his feet or legs and simply hoped that these waters were not infested with anything that might like a bite of him.

'I'll tell you what, Radar,' Billy winced as something slimy brushed against his leg 'I almost wish Kwok would get on and bomb them. And the crocodiles. Why can't they get that we're on the same side?'

After what seemed like at least an hour but was probably just ten minutes or so, Radar remarked:

'Is it just me or have they given up on us?' He peered around the boat and confirmed that there was no sign of mud men. He hauled himself back into the boat and then pulled Billy in, no easy feat, as both were slimy with mud and nervous about capsizing, complete with biscuit tin bomb.

While Radar checked over the bomb, Billy picked up one of the darts that had landed in the boat, rather gingerly. He was still half convinced that there was poison on the end of it. It had amazing brilliant green and scarlet feathers on the end. He pulled a couple out and stuck them behind his ears before throwing the dart overboard. They paddled on towards the landing place below the rock outcrop, relieved that the mud men had been seen off but still nervous about what was yet to come.

Billy pushed the boat as far between the two rocks as he could while Radar unwrapped the biscuit tin from its waterproof packing. Billy was happy enough leaving the bomb to Radar. The heat was even more stifling now that they were on dry land – hopefully it wouldn't set the thing off somehow. Billy had horrible visions of some sort of spontaneous combustion. As they reached the mossy rock that led to the secret entrance, he could only think how cool and inviting it looked.

'I'd better go in first as I'm the one that has to detonate this thing,' Radar turned to Billy but then burst into a bout of uncontrolled laughter. 'What the devil do you look like?'

'You don't look so great yourself!' It was true – both boys were covered top to toe in dried mud from their little encounter with the natives of Ybur.

Billy followed Radar this time, through the tunnel with its now familiar mushroomy smell and ever-narrowing twists and turns. The heat and brightness of the outside world became muffled in cool, musty darkness. Billy's thoughts were fixed on the immediate: he stooped as Radar stooped, crouched as Radar crouched. Finally, he sunk down to his hands and knees on the soft, silt floor.

'Billy! Stop there a minute. And keep quiet!' Radar's whisper echoed through the deep brown nothingness. Billy stopped, on all fours. He heard Radar start a low groaning roar. There was silence. Then a deep purring sound answered. Radar roared once more, but this time for longer and with more urgency. An answer came from the dungeon ahead.

'Good, that's settled.' Radar's instant reversion to his human voice was a little uncanny. 'Now to get this incendiary device from deepest Surrey on the go...'

'D'you know what you're doing?'

'I rather hope so...Pater showed me how to do it by feel...there's a fuse here somewhere...have to feed it through the hole in the tin...you're best getting right back now as I'm going to have to go like the clappers once it's lit...you'll need to get into position for when it blows...arms around knees, head well out of the way...'

As Billy retreated, Radar edged forwards as far as he could, placing the biscuit tin in the narrowing tunnel ahead and then slithered backwards, taking the fuse with him.

'OK! Detonate!' Radar lit a match and with it the fuse. There seemed to be an unending time of cool and damp and still but then it came. A glorious almighty explosion as the tunnel thudded and pulsated, accompanied by the stink of burning sugar like a candyfloss machine on overdrive blowing up. And, strangely, the multi-decibel roar of a wild and furious tiger. In fact, the tiger's roaring persisted as the dust settled.

Billy felt grimy to the bone from the dust now coating the caked-on mud. His ears still pounded from the aftermath of the explosion. But ahead, there was Radar, silhouetted in daylight. The Peek Frean's bomb had done its job. They just had to get to Durga now before it was too late. Billy stuck one hand into his mud-covered shorts pocket to check on the key that Flt Sgt Singh had constructed.

'Good little diversion from Durga,' Radar grinned as they made their way into the light of the underground dungeon. 'I expect that the full racket of the blast would have been muffled a bit by Pa's silencer and all the earth in the tunnel but you never can be too sure.'

Billy led the way to the cells. In the third of these stood Durga, proud and defiant, her emerald eyes flashing. Radar approached her and stood in front of the cell, staring into her eyes while making a strange throaty noise. Durga lunged and growled, distrustful at first. Rather you than me, thought Billy. But, as Radar persisted, Durga's expression gradually changed to one of almost playful happiness and she rubbed herself through the bars against Radar's hand, like a giant ginger cat.

Billy was fascinated – he could have watched the beautiful creature for hours. But there was a mission to complete. He reached for the peculiar key contraption that

Radar's father had made from a coat hanger and some old radio parts. It had got muddy and full of grit during their adventures so he had to fiddle and fumble with it rather more than he expected in the ancient lock. As he tried yet again, this time turning the thing the other way around, Durga suddenly fell quiet. Her ears pricked up, alert.

Two sets of horribly familiar footsteps descended towards them. One set was firm and deliberate. The other was heavy and uneven, accompanied by a menacing, echoing thud.

'Billy!' hissed Radar. 'You have to get that lock open. We can't go back now!'

Billy rattled the key this way and that. Still nothing. He knew he had to concentrate on the lock but he could only focus on the ominous sound of those heavy steps coming closer and closer.

'One more twist…come *on!*' The lock was like one of those infuriating metal puzzles that suddenly fall apart in your fingers when you least expect them to. And, when he least expected, Billy felt something click into place. 'Got it!' he yelled.

But at that moment, he looked up from the lock and over his right shoulder to the stairs. Two huge men appeared from the staircase. They seemed to fill the entire dungeon with their sheer size. On the right was the bodyguard, tall, hefty and shaven-headed with an apelike face and a jutting jaw. On the left, closer to Billy and Durga's cage stood General Kwok. Kwok was also tall but his enormous girth made him appear shorter than the bodyguard. His scarlet uniform with gold epaulettes seemed incongruous in the dark and dusty dungeon. His gigantic hand grasped a cane encrusted with rubies and other jewels.

Billy stared, wide-eyed and frozen to the spot. But the reaction from Kwok and his henchman was totally unexpected. The two colossi stopped, their jaws dropped and four eyes became transfixed with fear:

'Uurrrr...aaarrgh!' The bodyguard's unintelligible scream echoed in Billy's ears as the shaven-headed giant turned and fled back up the stairs. Billy was left staring at General Kwok, pinned against the wall, paralysed.

It struck Billy at just the point that Radar whispered to him: what the villains could see were two small figures, almost naked and caked in white mud, one of whom had feathers in his hair – 'they think we're the mud men!'

Billy narrowed his eyes and fixed General Kwok with his gaze:

'Haaarrrr!' Billy growled, baring his teeth.

The massive general's bottom lip began to tremble and he clutched hold of the wall beside him, dropping the bejewelled cane. It rolled across the dungeon floor towards Radar, who grabbed it and advanced, brandishing the cane at Kwok. Billy quickly flipped open the huge lock on Durga's cell. Radar turned to Durga and growled something in tiger-speak. Durga needed no prompting. She padded slowly and stealthily towards Kwok. Her emerald eyes were fixed on his face, which was twisted with equal measures of fear and fury.

Then, with a surprising agility given his size and handicap, General Kwok turned his huge bulk around and tried to run back up the stairs, following in the footsteps of his bodyguard. But, with his supporting cane gone, he tripped on the second step and collapsed as his entire weight fell on his old wound:

'Aaaarrrr...au...au...aaargh!'

'Get up, man!' Radar barked. Wielding the cane while stroking Durga's head, he signalled to Kwok to get into the cell. Kwok hauled himself up, his eyes blazing, his teeth clenched in pain, the ruby set in his front tooth glistening like blood, and staggered into the cell. He flopped down on his side, breathing heavily, perhaps grateful to be at least safe from Durga.

Billy was just re-securing the lock when more footsteps on the stairs made him jump. Footsteps that he recognised – hard and metallic. And before they had time to run or react, Oswald Featherstonehaugh swooped into the dungeon, pointing a revolver straight at Durga:

'Stop right there or the pussycat gets it. Hands up!'

Chapter 9

The Indian cobra

Billy and Radar obeyed, dropping the cane and the key in the process. Billy bit his lip. If only they'd turned and run while they could – they would have got away, he was sure of it. Now what was going to happen? Featherstonehaugh stood back on his heels, surveying the scene now that he had control. Durga growled and Radar muttered something: soft, yet urgent. Featherstonehaugh flinched, his eyes darting to Radar, but he quickly regained his composure:

'Well, well. Most interesting. If it isn't Johnny Walker's little sidekick, playing at Boy's Own Adventures! Your rather ingenious disguise may well have fooled General Kwok and his bodyguard – and the General *is* on strong medication – but there's no fooling me.' Featherstonehaugh took a step towards Billy. 'I know you from the airliner,' he hissed in a breath of acrid cigarettes. 'No mud man has baby blue eyes, my boy.'

Billy turned to Radar to avoid Featherstonehaugh's glare. Durga snarled, baring ferocious, powerful teeth. Radar stroked her head, desperately trying to keep her at bay. He was no doubt terrified that Featherstonehaugh would act on his word and shoot her, but Billy was just as worried about what an enraged Durga might do – to any of them. The gun still trained on Durga, Featherstonehaugh looked up from Billy and turned his attention to Radar:

'And who's your strange chum here? Mowgli?'

'My name is Singh.'

'Oh, speak English, do you? Good. Let's stick to that, then, so that we can all understand. No more of that mumbo-jumbo. Otherwise…well!' Featherstonehaugh moved the gun in Durga's direction. Durga reacted with a threatening forepaw lunge. Featherstonehaugh sprang backwards and fixed his angry gaze on Radar:

'Your job, Mowgli, is to make damned sure that the pussycat behaves herself until we get her locked up again…as is right and proper for such a beast – don't you agree?' At this point a grunting and cursing came from the cell and Featherstonehaugh noticed General Kwok for what seemed the first time.

'Ah, my most excellent General! I am sorry to see you in such a predicament. I'm afraid that I feel only shame that the offspring of one of my countrymen has brought such pain to the illustrious General Kwok. But now, General, I'm sure you'll agree that my services to your country and to your excellent person are worth every gold ingot and more that you have already so generously paid me.' He turned back to the boys and the tiger and snorted a contemptuous laugh. 'So the big hero Squadron Leader Johnny Walker gets babes-in-arms to do his dirty work, these days. Doubtless he's lounging around at this very moment being fanned by his Gupta and sipping on a pink gin. Is that someone to be proud of, boy?'

'What do you intend to do with us…and the tiger?' Radar asked.

'I'd advise you to call me Sir if you have any further questions, Mowgli. First, we're going to play musical chairs. You, Baby Blue Eyes, can unlock this cell and help the good General Kwok to his feet and out. And you can lock up that beast and your peculiar chum there in his place. So, move!'

Reluctantly, Billy picked up the key from the dungeon floor. It felt slippery in his hand. He fumbled at the lock of the cell and felt no sense of elation when the lock sprung open again.

'Here you are, General,' Billy offered the cane to General Kwok. He could hardly bear to look the terrifying and furious man in the eyes, feeling almost guilty for having tricked him.

'How *dare* you, boy!' The cane came down hard across his knuckles as the General lashed out. Billy winced. 'And now I'm away to have my medication. A triple dose…and I won't be responsible for any consequences that *that* has!'

Billy's eyes followed Kwok as he stomped up the stairs, seething and muttering:

'Tricked. By a couple of damned schoolboys…'

Featherstonehaugh's nasal voice dragged Billy's attention back to Radar's predicament. Featherstonehaugh cocked his head in the direction of the cell to Radar, spitting out the words:

'Stop gawping around…this isn't a circus. I said move! And take that monster with you, Mowgli, seeing as you're so pally. I'll decide what to do with you later.' Radar muttered something into the snarling Durga's ear then strode into the cell, flashing a look of defiance back at Featherstonehaugh. Featherstonehaugh motioned to Billy to lock the door:

'…And throw that confounded key contraption on the ground when you're done. You can never be too careful, especially with *his* sort.' Billy dropped the key by the door with a sullen scowl. Featherstonehaugh kicked it away and checked the lock, eyes still blazing at Radar. Durga growled and bared her teeth.

'…Keep that damned beast under control with whatever bloody witch-doctoring tricks you know!' Billy glanced up at Featherstonehaugh: was that a hint of fear amid the bluster?

'And now,' Featherstonehaugh drew back from the cage, pulling Billy with him, 'we're going to play a bit of "Tell Uncle Oswald", boy. I need information. About RAF Botawaddy. And specifically about the planes. And you're going to tell me. Because, if you don't, your furry friend over there will roar her last.'

Billy felt sick and dizzy. Featherstonehaugh had grabbed the back of his head by the hair with his free hand and was pulling at his scalp, forcing him to look up into his twisted, sneering face. Billy longed to spit into that evil face or to run his foot down Featherstonehaugh's shin and follow-up with a stamp, as he'd seen in a self-defence book, but he had no shoes on and he was terrified as to what his captor might do.

'Firstly, I need to know if those Botawaddy chummies have got anything other than clapped-out museum pieces and trainer kites there. Anything interesting and up-to-date? Any jet fighters? Hmm?'

'Don't tell him, Billy,' Radar hissed through the bars of the cell.

'I don't really know...Sir. I mean, we came here in a helicopter this time...'

'And the last time that you were snooping around here with Mowgli in places that don't concern you?'

Without thinking how on earth Featherstonehaugh knew about their previous expedition, Billy answered:

'Well, that was a little plane that time...a Chipmunk...a trainer kite, like you said...Sir.'

'That's as maybe but I'm sure that Squadron Leader Johnny Walker won't have been able to resist showing off a proper plane or two to his little admirers. What have they got there and where is it kept? Have you, for instance, seen a Hawker Hunter there? Now, Baby Blue Eyes, think carefully and quickly...or else I pull the trigger...'

Billy, confused and panicking, tried to shut Featherstonehaugh's voice out of his mind. He must *think*.

'Well?' Featherstonehaugh yanked at Billy's hair. Billy automatically turned his head to one side. He caught a glimpse of something – or was it someone? – crouching in the shadows in the dungeon's way out, exactly where he had crouched 24 hours earlier.

'Sir...look! There's something there...past the cage...you can see...in the shadows, there!'

'Humph! What do you take me for, boy? Let's forget the silly playground distraction manoeuvres, shall we? You were just about to tell me. Is there a Hawker Hunter at Botawaddy? Well?' Featherstonehaugh dragged Billy back towards the cell and pointed the gun straight at Durga's head. He grinned a nasty lopsided smirk and motioned the gun at Durga, making a clicking noise with his tongue.

Suddenly, Featherstonehaugh screamed out, his eyes right in Billy's, the revolver poised:

'*Have they got a Hawker Hunter?*'

'Yeah, yeah – there's a Hawker Harrier there!' In desperation, Billy blurted out the first thing that came into his mind without telling the truth.

'A Hawker what?' Featherstonehaugh almost spat into Billy's face, but his eyes were wild and gleaming.

'Hu…Ha…whatever you said,' Billy trembled, realising that the Harrier would still have been in prototypes and testing and probably Official Secrets back here in 1962.

'Harrier! But how could *you* know, Baby Blue Eyes…' still yanking Billy's hair and keeping the gun poised on Durga, Featherstonehaugh stared into the caverns of the dungeon. Then, he seemed to compose himself. He looked Billy deep into the eyes, bringing the revolver up to his forehead:

118

'I feel there is more to you than meets the eye, boy. Harrier, you said. You and I need a little talk. Away from Mowgli and his Jungle Book friend here. Now, get up those stairs where we can discuss everything in private!'

Billy flung a last glance at Radar and Durga in the cell as he was hustled up the stairs by Featherstonehaugh and his revolver. And out of the corner of his eye, he could again see the vague outline of an animal – or could it be a human figure? – crouching in the shadows. He managed a quick signal in that direction to Radar before Featherstonehaugh cuffed his hand away and they turned the corner in the stairs leading to the unknown interior of General Kwok's palace.

There seemed to be miles of twisting stairs and corridors. Cold stone turned into warm and sumptuous carpet, every inch of which he felt with his bare feet. And finally, Featherstonehaugh pushed Billy into a vast domed room:

'Take a seat and make yourself comfortable for our little chat.' He shoved Billy towards a dark, carved wooden chair. Billy sat nervously, and flinched as Featherstonehaugh strode towards him, brandishing a pair of handcuffs.

'Hands behind your back!' Featherstonehaugh snarled. The handcuffs clicked shut. Billy breathed in deeply, inhaling the obnoxious smell of the room: stale cigar smoke and strong alcohol, mixed in with some strange oriental incense. As Featherstonehaugh turned his attention to a drinks cabinet, splashing a good measure of whisky from a decanter into a glass and lighting one of his vile-smelling and all-too-familiar cigarettes, Billy swallowed, sat back in the chair and glanced around the room.

Above him was a high, domed roof, partly made from glass, out of which one could presumably gaze across the lake and into the skies. An ornate but dusty chandelier hung on a heavy chain from the ceiling. The room itself, although vast, was cluttered and over-furnished. The walls were hung with leopard skins and Billy noticed a number of other hunting trophies on display: an elephant's foot in which were a collection of silvered and bejewelled canes, numerous elephant tusks, a stuffed crocodile and a number of skulls of apes and monkeys. He felt queasy: his fear, the sense of menace in this room full of dead creatures and the stink of Featherstone's cigarette and neat whisky all combined to make him gag. He turned his head away from the smoke. But it was then that his eyes rested on something even worse than the skins and heads. In a glass tank on a circular table in the middle of the room writhed a live snake – a cobra.

'Right!' Featherstonehaugh took a slurp of his whisky and banged the heavy tumbler down on a dark wooden sideboard. 'Hawker Harrier, eh? It's time we got to know each other. Who are you, exactly?'

'I'm...Squadron Leader Walker's nephew, Billy. Over from England.'

'And your full name is...'

Billy desperately wanted to have time to think but realised how unnatural that would look. His real surname? No, that might cause problems:

'William James Walker.' He tried to sound confident.

'A bit of "Sir", wouldn't go amiss,' Featherstonehaugh blew smoke out of the twisted corner of his mouth into Billy's face. 'William James Walker. Squadron Leader Walker's nephew. So that's your Uncle Johnny,' Featherstonehaugh spoke in a patronising way, as if to a much younger child. 'Let's continue this story of Happy Families. Whose brother is he?' With the last question, his voice quickened and he lunged towards Billy, staring him straight in the eyes.

'My mum's...Sir.' Billy blurted out, without thinking. This answer obviously pleased Featherstonehaugh greatly. He sat back against the sideboard, took a sip of whisky and savoured it before speaking:

'Oh, dearie-me! A scandal in the Happy Family. And, William James Walker, don't you find that just a touch embarrassing? That you're a little bas...'

'What?' Billy, in panic, was wondering what on earth he'd said. 'What do you mean, embarrassing?'

Featherstonehaugh smirked. 'That you were born out of wedlock, my blue-eyed boy.' Seeing the confused expression on Billy's face, he continued, raising his voice. 'That your mother isn't married...or perhaps that doesn't matter wherever it is you come from...'

'She *is*! She just kept her...unmarried name or whatever it's called!' Billy realised what Featherstonehaugh was driving at but he wasn't sure whether he was digging himself even deeper into the hole in which he was trapped.

'Well, that's most novel!' Featherstonehaugh snorted. 'What is she? A film star, perhaps?' Before Billy had time to answer, another question was fired at him:

'And what's your date of birth?'

Still tangled up in the question of uncles and Walkers and maiden names, Billy was taken by surprise. He blurted out his birthday, hoping that would give him time to think.

'Year?' Featherstonehaugh barked, threateningly.

'Nineteen sixty...I mean nineteen seventy...no, fifty...um...five. Sir.'

'Bit of a big boy for six, aren't you?' Featherstonehaugh sneered triumphantly. Billy knew that he was found out. He slumped back in the uncomfortable chair, trying to avoid Featherstonehaugh's glance. His mind was on overdrive. What could he tell Featherstonehaugh? The truth? Would that be believed? What had Featherstonehaugh in mind for him, anyway?

'So, Billy Blue-Eyes is *not* who he claims to be,' Featherstonehaugh finished his whisky almost thoughtfully, stood up and started to wander around the room. He picked up a monkey skull and turned it over in his hands. When he spoke, it was addressed to no one in particular:

'But who is he? Where is he from? And why? Tell me...' he threw down the skull and rounded on Billy again. 'Why *did* Walker bring you over?'

'To be chums with Rad...young Singh.'

'A deuced peculiar notion of Walker's. What on earth could you possibly have in common with a boy like that?'

'He's my friend!' Despite his precarious position, Billy was furious.

'If I were you,' Featherstonehaugh remarked dismissively, continuing his slow pacing of the room. 'I'd be a little more selective in my choice of friends. The likes of Mowgli won't come to anything – not in the civilized world, at any rate. But I digress...we were going to find out who you really are...and we appear to have all the time in the world at our disposal.' He paused ominously at the snake tank. 'Frightened of snakes, are you?'

'No more than anyone else, Sir.' Billy hoped that the "Sir" would prompt Featherstonehaugh to move on but he didn't. Instead, to Billy's horror, Featherstonehaugh reached inside the tank and carefully pulled out the cobra, stroking its head. He moved a few steps towards Billy, who automatically sunk down in the chair.

'You have good enough cause to be frightened of this little devil. An Indian cobra. It's highly toxic. Within six hours of a bite the victim dies most unpleasantly through suffocation caused by paralysis of the diaphragm. A slow and painful death.' Featherstonehaugh chuckled suddenly. 'I expect you wish your chum Mowgli was here. I'm sure that he's quite proficient at snake charming. His sort usually are.' He took a couple of steps towards Billy, who could do nothing other than stare, transfixed with terror, at the cobra. Its menacing hood loomed and its forked tongue lashed. But then Featherstone-haugh turned suddenly, dropped the creature in its tank, brushed his hands off against his trousers and lit another cigarette.

'So, you see, my boy. It's all quite simple. You will tell me everything I want to know. And, if you don't tell me, you can answer to the Indian cobra. And I'm damned sure that not only the thought of the slow lingering pain of its poison but also the realisation that you might never see your parents again – whoever they may be – will get your tongue wagging. I return to my original subject. What did you mean by a Hawker Harrier?'

Billy sighed. He was slightly less terrified now that the snake was back in its tank and that the interrogation had gone back to aircraft. And, was it possible? His hands had sweated so much that he was convinced that, with a bit of wriggling, he might just be able to slide one hand out of the adult-size handcuffs. But he'd have to choose his moment. The thought gave him courage and jogged his memory to something Grandpop had explained about Featherstonehaugh as they drove through the summer countryside in the Austin Healey. Something about his name...

'I ...really don't know, Mister Feather-Stone-Haw!'

'*What* did you call me?' Featherstonehaugh jumped towards Billy, looking as if he was about to strangle him. Simultaneously, Billy wrenched first one, then the other sweaty hand free of the handcuffs. But Billy's escape and Featherstonehaugh's fury were suddenly eclipsed by a crashing and shattering sound from the domed ceiling above. Billy stared above as glass showered down. And then he heard a familiar voice.

Chapter 10

Duel in the dome

'Fanny Featherstonehaugh, I presume!' Grandpop swung into the room from above, amid a shower of broken glass. As Featherstonehaugh turned to confront the sudden intruder, Billy freed himself from the chair and scuttled into a corner of the room.

'Well damn you, Walker!' blustered Featherstonehaugh. 'You have a talent for turning up when you're not wanted.' He reached for his revolver but Grandpop launched into a jump kick, sending the weapon spinning across the floor towards Billy's corner, colliding with the shards of broken glass. Billy crouched motionless, as if he was still handcuffed to the chair. But his eyes were glued to the fallen revolver.

'Not wanted?' scoffed Grandpop. 'Now, come on, Mr Featherstonehaugh. If you're so keen to see RAF Botawaddy and our planes I'd be more than happy to escort you. We can even take back the kite you borrowed...'

'Hah! You can go to blazes, Walker! You think you can parachute in and play the big hero but you seem to forget who you're dealing with here!' Featherstonehaugh lunged at Grandpop and grabbed his neck with both hands. Grandpop reacted quickly, scraped his boot down Featherstonehaugh's shin and followed up with a punch under his jaw. His opponent lost his footing for a second but came back with his right fist into Grandpop's cheek. Grandpop collapsed backwards into the sideboard. A few glasses and the decanter of whisky crashed to the floor. The sudden stink of alcohol bit at the back of Billy's throat as he crouched, transfixed on the fight and on the revolver: so near and yet so far...

The massive throne room throbbed with aggressive energy, deflecting like lightning from the broken glass. Featherstonehaugh seized an ornamental sword from the wall. He drew it from its silver and ruby sheath. Brandishing it with a malevolent chuckle, he advanced towards Grandpop. Grandpop, cornered against the sideboard where he'd fallen, grabbed a cane from the elephant's foot on the floor beside him. He leapt to his feet.

'Just as well that I grew up watching Errol Flynn!' Grandpop joked and flung a grin in Billy's direction. Niftily, he dodged his approaching opponent and darted around the room, fending off Featherstonehaugh's lunges with the heavy sword:

'And what exactly is your little game here?' Grandpop sprung onto the wooden chair that had recently seated a terrified Billy. 'What have you done with your rather corpulent chum Kwok?' Grandpop leapt at Featherstonehaugh and drove him towards the wall.

'None of your damned business, Walker. Or the RAF's. Or are you under the illusion that Ybur is still part of the glorious British Empire?' Featherstonehaugh aimed a thrust of the sword but Grandpop responded quickly. He blocked with the cane and kicked the elephant's foot into Featherstonehaugh's path. Featherstonehaugh stolpered against the thing, which set him momentarily off-guard amid a loud volley of cursing.

Billy took the opportunity to inch forward to where Featherstonehaugh's revolver was lying amongst the broken glass. If he could only get it…but now Featherstonehaugh had the same idea. His free hand grasped behind him, trying to reach the weapon, although his eyes were still trained on Grandpop. Quickly, Billy took advantage of the situation. He kicked the revolver out of Featherstonehaugh's reach, then shrunk back into his corner again as the man's agile frame swooped dangerously close in a renewed attack on Grandpop.

Grandpop leapt onto a solid oak desk and launched himself into a magnificent swing across the room on the chandelier. He aimed his heavy boots straight at Featherstonehaugh, who was sent hurtling into the wall.

Various stuffed heads of long-dead jungle beasts crashed to the ground in a confusion of dusty violence.

With Featherstonehaugh temporarily grounded, Billy took another chance to help Grandpop. He slunk out towards where the gun was lying, in a pool of glass splinters, under the circular table with the cobra tank. His mouth was dry, his heart seemed to be on fast-forward and his eyes were blinded by the sunlight streaming in from the broken windows. So perhaps it wasn't surprising that what happened next all seemed to take place in dreadful slow motion.

Featherstonehaugh loomed up again like a furious cobra and threw his entire energy into a massive lunge at Grandpop, who had retrieved his cane. Grandpop ducked backwards out of the way. But this gave Featherstonehaugh the chance he needed. He slammed his sword down on the reptile tank.

The tank smashed. Billy was transfixed. The cobra was out! Much worse, it was slithering towards him, enraged. Perhaps… perhaps, if he didn't move one single muscle, it would go away. But now his hands, tensed and sweaty, started shaking. The cobra was not fooled. Intent and angry, it reared up in front of him, hood flaring.

Billy cowered, trapped. If only he could control this shaking. He must keep quiet…calm…as still as he possibly could. He glanced over at Grandpop, instinctively, for help. Grandpop would get him out of this. But his eyes met a look he had not yet seen on Grandpop's face: the indecision when faced with a terrible choice. Like Billy, Grandpop was speechless, frozen to the spot, eyes fixed on the terrifying snake. Featherstonehaugh had withdrawn towards the door. He rested his sword on the sideboard, lit one of his foul cigarettes and gloated with evil pleasure at the scene:

'Nice little dilemma for you, Walker. I don't suppose they taught you how to get out of *that* one at the Staff College. Try and bag me or save your nephew from my serpentine pal there? Remember, any sudden movement or loud noise and our hooded friend will strike!' Featherstonehaugh spoke in a soft hiss through a cloud of cigarette smoke. 'Oh, and by the way…if you do manage to extricate yourselves, I wouldn't mind you introducing me to your sister one of these days. Sounds a racy kind of gel. Although I'd say her decision to leave her offspring in your tender care was a trifle misjudged. Well, three's a crowd as they say so I think I'll make myself scarce at this point. Toodle-pip!' And Featherstonehaugh nonchalantly cast his still-lit cigarette end on the floor, blew a last puff of smoke out of the side of his curling lips, turned on his heel and swept out of the room.

'You rotten, despicable coward...' Grandpop whispered through gritted teeth. He turned to Billy. Billy crouched, his arms wrapped around his knees, his eyes glued in terror on the cobra's own beady black eyes. 'Now, old chap, just keep still,' Grandpop spoke softly and slowly. 'I'll get you out of this. Don't make any sudden movements ... these devils try to preserve their venom at all costs...'

Billy gulped even though his mouth was dry. He was petrified that the slightest little whimper, the slightest twitch would further enrage the snake. It stood, its hood flared menacingly, not more than an arm's length away from him. And as he gulped, his nostrils breathed in the smell of burning. Featherstonehaugh's discarded cigarette had set a trail of spilt whisky alight and growing flames now crept across the floor. Billy buried his head in his knees in terrified despair. He could hear Grandpop's voice moving closer and closer to him. He tried to make himself so small and insignificant that he would disappear. Although he couldn't risk looking up, he could sense, with a terrible clarity, that the cobra's path away from him was now blocked by fire. And that the two of them, snake and boy, were trapped in a deadly duel of nerves.

And now all was quiet. Grandpop's whisper had stopped. A slight breeze swept into the hellishly hot room and the floor throbbed slightly, as if from a heavy but silent set of footsteps.

'Billy, old chap...look up...but stay mum...that's the boy...' Grandpop's voice was encouraging as Billy very slowly lifted his head and opened his eyes. The cobra was still there, and the fire. But beyond this, towards the door, emerald green eyes in a stripy face met Billy's gaze: Durga! Followed by Radar, the huge tiger padded softly and carefully into the room. Grandpop signalled to Radar, pointing in Billy's direction. Billy's heart leapt as his attention was finally distracted away from his own predicament. He almost cried out to his friend but had to bite his tongue.

Radar whispered something in Durga's ear. The tiger crept stealthily from the door, across the broken glass and around the fire to where Grandpop was standing. Grandpop seemed to understand instinctively that the big cat was going to succeed where he could only have tried. He nodded to Durga's animal superiority as he slipped quietly around the room to join Radar near the door. Billy watched, frozen in the heat, only his eyes flitting from the cobra, to Grandpop, to the trail of fire, to Radar – and to Durga. He *had* to trust her, now. This was his only chance. His glance returned to the snake and stayed locked there. He mustn't move. He must not even blink...

It took Billy completely by surprise. Durga roared. The cobra turned, flared its hood and bared its fangs. The deadly poisonous venom shot across the broken glass and flames towards the emerald eyes of the tiger. And Durga leapt with the speed and agility of a gazelle back to her human rescuer at the door.

'Billy!' Grandpop and Radar shouted in chorus as Billy sprang, released and suddenly charged with some unknown power, over fire, over broken glass, over fallen animal heads and a capsized elephant's foot to the door and safety at last. Radar quickly ushered Billy and Durga out of the throne-room into the corridor outside. Grandpop grabbed Featherstone-haugh's discarded revolver from the floor and pulled the door to smartly.

'Wow, Radar!' Billy just stared at his friend in disbelief. 'How did you…I mean, you were locked up in that cell down there, with Durga…what…'

'It's a long story and one I'm not sure you'd believe …there's certainly no time for it just now,' Radar turned to Grandpop who nodded, smiling. 'Let's just say…we've got a new ally in our fight against Kwok…a mud man called Mani…and he's out to get Kwok with a vengeance as we speak…he's gone to…'

Grandpop cut Radar off kindly but firmly as the odd-assorted group stood at the top of the palace staircase. 'Now, first of all, jolly good show, Radar, and you, Durga – what a beautiful pussy you are, if I may say so! And young Billy, of course, for not losing your bottle in there. But we're not through yet. I suggest we divide and conquer. We have Featherstonehaugh about to make off with our Sunderland. We have a mud man on his own, as I understand it, against Kwok and his henchmen. And we have a deadly reptile plus the potential of an inferno behind this door. Flight is waiting overhead in the chopper. I suggest, Radar, that you get yourself, Billy and Durga outside to him asap, while I…'

'But Squadron Leader! Mani…the mud man…I can't just leave him…he rescued us from that blasted cage, for God's sake…' Radar spoke with passion and urgency.

Grandpop narrowed his eyes. 'Good. You can take responsibility for getting him out of here. Take Durga with you but for goodness' sake no heroics or going after Kwok. God only knows what state he's in or how many of his damned bodyguard beasts are still at large. What happens to him is by the by. Get your mud man chum out of here at the double. And Billy will come with me to reacquisition the Sunderland. Remember. The fire is contained now behind the door but it could erupt at any moment. Time is of the essence. Is that clear?'

'Yes, Sir!' Radar saluted and bent down to whisper something to Durga.

'Good. We'll re-group outside when we're done. Airlift from Flight. And, good luck!'

Radar and Durga leapt down the winding ornate staircase, in a kaleidoscope of tanned and stripy legs. As they disappeared, Grandpop grinned at Billy, ruffled his hair and signalled at him to follow them down the stairs:

'That got a little hairy back there,' he said, his voice punctuated by their feet clattering down the stairs, 'think I'll stick to being a pilot. Zookeeper is no job for me! I'm not over keen on creepy-crawlies, either, old chap. Right – we're going to have to get a move on if we want to catch up with our Sunderland. Seems highly likely that Featherstonehaugh is going to try and do a bunk in her!'

As Billy's legs pounded down the twisting stairway, which was hung with ruby and sapphire-covered chandeliers, a huge sense of relief swept over him, propelling him down and down, with purpose. His attention was on the here-and-now, which was June 1962 in Ybur, and not on how he might (or might not) get back to his own time. Just as in a dream, you never start wondering how, when and if you are going to wake up, so it was with Billy. Ybur had become his reality.

Grandpop and Billy rushed down the staircase, through the spectacular entrance hall of Kwok's palace and out into the blinding heat of the tropical mid-day. They galloped down a flight of shining white steps to a wooden jetty. It was clear that a motorboat had recently departed: the smell of fuel and a distant buzz hung in the air.

Chapter 11

Fight in the flying boat

'Quick!' Grandpop yelled to Billy. 'Jump aboard that dinghy – we'll have to row out there.' They made their way over the bright turquoise water to where the Sunderland was moored, like a majestic white seabird. Featherstonehaugh had tied the motorboat to the pontoon and his slim figure could just be seen hoisting itself up through the portside door. Grandpop rowed faster, with urgency as Billy sat in the prow of the dinghy, cool water splashing in his face, rope at the ready.

They drew nearer. Billy heard the sound of engines starting up. As they reached the pontoon, the four propellers were already spinning. Billy and Grandpop quickly leapt out of the boat onto the pontoon and burst through the door of the flying boat. Before they could do anything, both were thrown across the floor of the lower deck as the fuselage lurched forward through the lake.

'Hold on for a tick. It's going to be a bit dicey – we're taking off!' gasped Grandpop. Billy grabbed hold of a door handle. Featherstonehaugh had already pulled the flying boat's nose out of the water and begun to climb. Billy felt his stomach turning around in all sorts of directions that it shouldn't as the Sunderland climbed jerkily into the sky.

'Does Featherstonehaugh know what he's doing with one of these?' Billy whispered.

'Debateable,' muttered Grandpop. 'Now, you follow me. We'll take him by surprise!' Billy felt the aircraft beginning to level off. Quietly, they climbed the ladder from the gunroom to the cockpit. Grandpop stealthily crept up behind Featherstonehaugh, who sat in the pilot's seat, intent at the controls. Then, with a small but decisive movement, Grandpop held the revolver to the side of Featherstonehaugh's face and hissed in his ear:

'Game's up, Fanny. Now do as I say. You're going to fly this kite back to where you stole it. Once you're up to three angels you need to bank and turn due west. And I'm going to sit in the dickie seat here and help you to navigate, just in case you've forgotten the way.'

Featherstonehaugh started to perspire. He didn't look at Grandpop but stared grimly ahead, his hand tightly gripping the central column. Billy felt uneasy. He was sure that Featherstonehaugh would not give in as easily as that.

'Right. Bear west!' Grandpop snapped at Featherstone-haugh and thrust the gun closer to his head. But

Featherstonehaugh suddenly pushed the central column forward with all his strength and the machine started to go into a dive.

'I'll take you down with me, damn you, Walker!' Featherstonehaugh screamed. 'And that bloody brat of yours...or whoever the hell he is!'

Grandpop threw down the gun and grabbed the central column, wrestling with it and with Featherstonehaugh, who was determined to crash into the water. The Sunderland bounced and juddered. One moment Grandpop had control, the next, Featherstonehaugh. Billy remembered some bad turbulence once on a flight back from holiday in Greece but this was ten thousand times worse. The whole plane shook and rattled and lurched around in three dimensions. Billy flinched as Featherstonehaugh jabbed his elbow into Grandpop's face. Grandpop responded with a powerful kick to Featherstonehaugh's thigh and grabbed the central column. Featherstonehaugh was sent crashing onto his back. Strangely, he did not spring back up. And then Billy saw with horror that Featherstonehaugh was reaching for his revolver, which was lying on the cockpit floor. Billy leapt up and kicked it towards Grandpop.

Grandpop grabbed the revolver and stood up from the pilot seat. He pointed the gun at Featherstonehaugh. Billy sprang into the vacant seat and grabbed the central column.

'Good show Billy, old chap. Don't get into a flap. Just hold her steady. That's the boy. I'm going to make Mr Featherstonehaugh here a deal,' Grandpop said, firmly.

Billy wasn't so calm. It took most of his strength to hold the central column steady. He didn't like to think how many tons of flying boat were suddenly under his control.

'Here's the deal,' Grandpop held the gun on Featherstonehaugh. 'Either you give yourself up and come back with us to RAF Botawaddy...'

'Never!' Featherstonehaugh roared. 'You won't take me alive, Walker!'

'...or,' Grandpop pointed the revolver straight between Featherstonehaugh's eyes, 'you can bale out. Now.' Featherstonehaugh turned and looked nervously down the ladder towards the gunroom and the door.

'That's right, old boy. The exit is there. Go ahead if you've got the guts for it. I don't suppose your chum General Kwok will want you back, after you've deserted him once...'

'I don't need that fat fool. I have enough in advance payments!'

'Well, go then! That's the way out. To the mud men. To whatever's lurking in that lake. Now damn well bale out before I change my mind and shoot you!'

Featherstonehaugh cast one more fleeting sneer at Billy and Grandpop then disappeared down the ladder. A blast of wind hit them as the door opened. And then Grandpop was back, sitting beside Billy at the controls.

'Good riddance!' Grandpop muttered and rubbed his cheek where a fine bruise was coming up. He seemed to have completely dismissed Featherstonehaugh and his full concentration now was on getting the Sunderland back on course. But Billy was astounded and had to have an answer:

'I...I just don't get it...why on earth did you... why did you let Featherstonehaugh go?'

Grandpop chuckled mysteriously. 'We go back a long way, Fanny and I. No, call it my sense of fair play if you like. He'll have to land somehow, and pit his wits against the jungle and the mud men but he had a 'chute on. I've given him a fighting chance.'

Billy was not a hundred percent satisfied but he let it go. The main thing now was that they'd got the plane back. And that for the first time in – how many hours? – he wasn't actually staring into the face of imminent death.

'Uncle Johnny...I mean Grandpop...thanks...really. For rescuing me and that...'

'The least I could do, old chap,' Grandpop grinned nonchalantly. 'And I didn't exactly do it single-handedly, either...'

'Yeah. If it hadn't been for Durga...and Radar. Oh, I do hope they're OK!'

'We'll soon see. Just have to get this bus landed – mission not yet completed!'

Grandpop pulled on the central column and manoeuvred the massive white bird back in the direction of the palace. Billy gazed out of the window as the plane banked around through the cloudless sky. As they began the descent, he caught sight of the Whirlwind hovering in the distance:

'Jolly good, there's Flight! Now, any sign on the ground of Singh *filius* or his feline companion?' Grandpop kept a tight grip on the controls as the flying boat came steadily nearer to the water.

Billy strained his eyes against the sun to see:

'No, I can't see them...but...oh, cripes! Grandpop, look! The palace is going up in flames!'

'Good God, you're right! Better get the old girl landed asap. Keep your eyes peeled for our chums...' Billy peered out of the window as they came in to land, willing Radar and Durga to appear. But all he could see were flames leaping from the broken windows of what must have been the throne-room into the freedom of the dazzling blue sky.

Grandpop landed the huge aircraft expertly on the water. As they leapt out onto the pontoon, Billy saw that the motorboat that Featherstonehaugh had used in his escape was no longer there.

'Looks like someone else has got the wind up and done a bunk. Probably Kwok's heavies couldn't stand the heat...' Grandpop waved up at the Whirlwind circling over the palace, indicating that they were on their way back with full speed. They sprung into the little dinghy and rowed flat-out back to the palace. Despite all Billy's willing and wishing, there was no sign of Radar, no sign of Durga. Just the ominous flames lashing ever more strongly at the brilliant blue sky.

Grandpop and Billy piled out of the dinghy and belted up the white entrance steps, glancing around all the while for their companions. As they reached the top, Grandpop paused and grabbed Billy's arm:

'Now, we've got to act quickly here but not do anything rash. No sign of Radar & Co. They could possibly have made it out to the back but I doubt it. We'll have to hope that blaze will be kept at bay for sufficient time for us to get them out. We need to make damn sure we don't open the door to that throne room. And we've got to be doubly on our guard here – we don't know for sure who's still around. Just stick right beside me. OK?' Billy nodded and spluttered from the smoke that hung in the air.

'Come on!' Grandpop gave Billy a reassuring nod as they crept swiftly into the palace. Billy followed Grandpop up the main staircase. They stopped every now and then to listen for Durga. Billy could feel the heat intensifying as they climbed higher and soon they came to the door of the domed room which remained – for now – reassuringly solid and closed. Grandpop paused and both wiped the sweat from their brows.

Just as Grandpop motioned him to go on, Billy felt something wet drip onto his right arm. He glanced down. A drop of blood glistened like a ruby on his skin. Horrified, he looked upwards. His glance met a huge body, slumped over the banister. He took in a shaved head and a massive gash to the throat, dripping blood like jewels from a macabre chandelier. With the delayed reaction that you get in dreams, Billy opened his mouth. But, before the scream came, a hand cupped over his mouth.

'Now, steady on, old chap. Not a pretty sight, I'll grant you, but he won't be doing us – or anyone else – any harm any more. But what happened to him? No yelling now, or we might be next.' Grandpop released his hand from Billy's mouth and the two of them continued stealthily up the ornate staircase. Although Billy desperately didn't want to look at the body as he went past, his curiosity got the better of him. His eyes darted in that direction for long enough to see that the lifeless bulk had once been Kwok's bodyguard. And as they passed the body, Billy heard a voice above them. He clutched Grandpop's arm. They both stopped and listened. The voice was an echoing deep booming. They could not hear distinct words but the tone was enraged and deranged.

'It's Kwok,' breathed Billy. 'Is he talking to himself?'

'One way to find out!' Grandpop whispered. They padded quietly up the stairs. The voice grew louder and more terrifying but it had a dreadful magnetic pull. They reached a closed door, stopped and listened. It was clear that General Kwok was in the room. And that he was not alone.

'Boy!' General Kwok's deep voice was slurred and indistinct but this made it all the more terrifying. 'Boy! You will kill the wild beast. You will thrust the knife into its heart. The beast will die!'

146

'No!' It was Radar's voice, full of desperation but defiant. 'No! You are completely deranged! You are mad and twisted by greed!'

A hollow, murderous laugh came from Kwok. He must be dosed up to the eyeballs on drugs, Billy thought. And Kwok's next utterance made it horribly clear what a desperate position Radar was in:

'Then...boy, I will cut the throat of this brave savage! Which is it to be? Man...or beast?'

'No! I don't believe you! You're bluffing!'

Kwok laughed, maniacally and horrifyingly. 'You have already witnessed the fate of the servant who dared to desert me! That was no bluff! Man ...or beast!'

'No!'

Billy couldn't take any more. This was hundreds of times worse than anything he'd experienced in the last few hours. Even the cobra. Here he was helpless, utterly powerless to save his friend. He willed something to happen, anything...please, Grandpop, please...

With a running jump Grandpop kicked the door down. For a nanosecond, Billy was confronted with a terrible scene. Kwok held a huge sabre to the throat of a young mud man. Radar, dagger in hand, stood defensively over Durga. Durga was poised to attack – who? As Grandpop sprang into the room, the momentarily frozen scene exploded into action. Durga leapt at Kwok with a roar, knocking his huge bulk to the ground. Kwok turned onto his hands and knees and Durga sank her teeth into his backside. Kwok let out an ear-splitting howl of agony that seemed to shake the whole palace. Implored by Radar, Durga released her grip on Kwok – but not before she had done painful damage, not to mention ripping a large stretch of scarlet material from the General's uniform trousers. Kwok fell back to the floor, writhing, quivering and sobbing, all vanity and arrogance gone. Durga surveyed the room, snarling and tense. Radar breathed soft, comforting words.

'Good show, that tiger,' added Grandpop, keeping a wary eye on Durga's reaction as he picked up Kwok's sabre. 'Young Singh…everything OK? That was a dashed awkward spot you found yourself in! And who is this chap?' Grandpop smiled and nodded at the young mud man, who was barely taller than Billy.

'His name's Mani. He's sixteen and his chief sent him on an initiation journey here. To prove his bravery.' Pride mixed with relief in Radar's voice.

'Well, it certainly looks as if he has done that!' Grandpop smiled respectfully at Mani. The young mud man grinned back, pointed at General Kwok, shook his head and drew his hand across his neck in a mock throat slitting.

'Absolutely!' Radar explained. 'Mani's tribe shot at us 'cos they thought we were in cahoots with Kwok but he followed us down the tunnel and when he saw how I am with Durga he realised we were friends. Tigers are sacred to Mani's people. So he unlocked the door! Together we managed to scare most of Kwok's entourage out of the palace…and then we found you…'

'Yes, and we've just seen Fanny Featherstonehaugh off!' Billy added. 'He's parachuted into the lake!' This exclamation was greeted by a pained groan from General Kwok, still lying on the floor of his chamber.

'Now, now,' Grandpop chuckled. 'No way to talk about your elders, though I hesitate to say betters. Complete bad sort, that Featherstonehaugh. But now that we *have* seen him off, we need to regroup and get ourselves back to Botawaddy. And, I don't want to cause undue alarm but there is the little matter of this palace being on fire as we speak. We need to move quickly. Radar: your Pater will be picking us up in the cab at the tradesman's entrance. I expect young Mani here will be eager to return to his people – and I think he's welcome to take proof that he's played a major role in preventing the destruction of his tribe at the hands of the so-called General.' Grandpop solemnly handed Mani Kwok's bejewelled cane. 'So, attention! Mani and Billy take the lead, then I'll follow up with our prisoner. We'll have to get our corpulent friend Mr Kwok down the tunnel but that shouldn't prove too difficult now that you chaps have blasted it open. And,' Grandpop cast a glance at Kwok who had been reduced to a sullen silence 'Mr Kwok will be followed up by young Singh on tiger duty and I'm sure our feline friend can give him the necessary encouragement to shift himself!'

The group trooped off as swiftly as they could, down from Kwok's chamber, past the closed door of the throne-room and back towards the dungeons and the tunnel. Billy thought how unlikely a procession they formed: two small figures – his own and Mani's – in the lead, followed by Kwok crawling on hands and knees spluttering and complaining about arson and betrayal, then Durga, closely followed by Radar, with Grandpop taking the rear. Kwok was none too keen on exiting his palace in such an undignified manner – on his hands and knees, with a torn uniform and bleeding bottom – and via a dusty old tunnel, too. But the odd growl from Durga and nudge with her nose kept him going in the right direction.

It wasn't long before they reached the open air. Mani's bark boat was tied alongside Billy and Radar's inflatable dinghy at the little bay. Billy grabbed the two T-shirts from the boat: how long was it exactly since they'd peeled them off in the hot sun? Full of pride and seemingly a few centimetres taller, Mani nodded and smiled to the strange group. He crouched down in front of Durga, closed his eyes, stretched out his arms and chanted some incantation in his own tongue. Then, with an agile bound, a broad grin and a wave of Kwok's cane, Mani leapt into his little boat. Billy and Radar watched the young mud man paddle away and gazed out across the sparkling surface of the lake.

'Featherstonehaugh must be out there somewhere...' Billy screwed his eyes up to try and catch a glimpse of anything moving. But once Mani and his boat disappeared into the horizon there were no signs of life on the lake. Luckily, there was a very clear sign of life in the sky: Flt Sgt Singh at the controls of the Whirlwind hovering above them. A ladder and a large crate were lowered down to the waiting party.

Grandpop patted the crate. 'This was originally intended for our stripy friend but...I think Mr Kwok here would appreciate his own private cabin...and we don't want him bleeding all over the chopper. Most nasty. Now, I'm sure you'll all excuse me if I take my leave at this point. I have stolen property to return. And I'd like to be alone with the old girl, for old time's sake!'

'Where *did* you learn all that stuff – talking to tigers and that?' Billy climbed up into the helicopter.

Radar smiled mysteriously: 'Let's just say it comes into the same category as your pictures of the lock. We've all got our talents…and they're not necessarily learned…' He whispered something into Durga's stripy ear as the Whirlwind soared high and triumphant above the deserted, burning palace.

Chapter 12

Durga, Rani and Rajah

Billy and Radar babbled "nineteen to the dozen," as Flt Sgt Singh put it, all the way back to RAF Botawaddy. Radar got to hear the full horror of Billy's ordeal in the throne-room, the Indian cobra and Featherstonehaugh's escape in complete graphic detail. And Radar gave Billy a hair-raising account of his adventures – culminating in the drug-crazed Kwok leaping on Mani with a huge sabre:

'He was out of his head on morphine and God knows what! Totally murderous. It was horrific. We were all locked in there with him and his drugged mad eyes and his lust for blood...' Radar shuddered.

'Wow! What d'you think they'll do with him? Will they hang him or something?' Billy asked, eyes wide.

'That would be too damned good for him!' Radar pounded his fist in his hand, furious at Kwok's inhumanity. 'I hope he rots in hell!'

'He most probably will, boys. Hell for Kwok, anyway. A prison with no luxuries, no splendid uniforms, no servants and lackeys, no mind-numbing drugs but just seconds, minutes, hours, days and years of dull empty time to fill up pondering his crimes…' Flt Sgt Singh allowed himself a small smile while he throttled down on the controls. The helicopter approached RAF Botawaddy. 'Of course the Wali of Ybur and representatives from Burmeon and the United Nations will be summoned and in due course he'll be given a fair trial. Which is more than he ever allowed any of his victims…'

General Kwok was duly deposited at RAF Botawaddy, patched up and locked up to await his fate once the Wali had been contacted and informed of his treachery.

Billy and Radar barely had time to recover their breath when Grandpop strode back into the compound from the direction of the lagoon. It wasn't quite time for the two of them to rest on their laurels.

'Come on, chaps, no time to lose. We have a family re-union to attend to once the monsoon blows over!'

After a satisfying meal of raw steak and plenty to drink, Durga was packed up in the crate recently vacated by General Kwok. Both Singhs advised that it was time to create some distance between tiger and humans if Durga was to be successfully returned to her natural habitat and – most importantly – her cubs.

'Even my...er...linguistic skills won't help if she thinks we're going to attack the little ones. It's instinct.' Radar grinned.

It was time to board the Westland Whirlwind again with Grandpop at the controls. Flt Sgt Singh and some of his colleagues stayed on the runway to ensure that the crate and its stripy cargo lifted up properly in the right direction. Radar and Billy sat with Grandpop. Radar was especially excited as he was allowed to navigate, having the best inside knowledge of where Durga had been captured.

'We need to fly due east towards our usual Ybur landing place but then northwards: it can't be more than six miles or so. There's a kind of plain, which turns quite quickly into dense jungle. And just near to where Durga was captured there are some temple ruins...this must be it!' Radar consulted the cloth map of Burmeon spread out over his knee. 'The ruined temple of Durga! It's even marked on here.'

It was a glorious afternoon. The monsoon had passed and the helicopter whirred above plains dense with dried grasses. Grandpop hummed an old-fashioned tune to himself while Billy peered down at the ground and at the crate swaying below them. Beyond the grasslands he saw the beginnings of forest and, in the distance, what looked like a clearing. He began to make out the ruins of an ancient temple. Huge pillars sprawled across the forest floor, overgrown with jungle green, looking like fallen and petrified tree trunks. There was something primeval and awe-inspiring about the spot: even as they drew in closer it was impossible to tell where man's work ended and nature began.

'Is that it?' Grandpop slowed the helicopter as Radar glanced from the map to the ground. 'Bingo!' he exclaimed excitedly.

'Righty-ho, chaps…' Grandpop gave them their orders. 'Let's get this operation properly co-ordinated. First, you'll disembark via rope ladder. Then, Billy, I suggest you scale a nearby tree to get to a position of safety. Radar – you are to deal with releasing our feline friend… then make yourself scarce, at the double, up same tree!'

Grandpop brought the Whirlwind down near to the ground in the clearing. Radar opened the hatch to let out a rope ladder. Billy clambered down first, into the busy, sticky heat, deafened by the buzz of the helicopter. Hanging onto the last rung, Billy glanced between his feet and saw a three metre drop, to ground that swung giddily in circles below him – but he landed well, on soft grasses. Radar followed and they set out to search for a tree that would provide the best and safest vantage point.

'Hey, Radar! I reckon this one will do nicely. Shouldn't be too tricky to climb either with all these vine things on it.' The tree was some twenty metres away from where the temple ruins sprouted out of the mossy undergrowth. Billy clambered up and settled into the higher branches. He gazed over at the ruins. His eyes were led up a crumbling stairway to an ancient door, guarded by tigers of stone. Here had once been power, and ceremony and spectacle. Now it had all been given over to the gentler but more lasting power of nature.

Sitting back against the trunk, his legs on either side of a sweeping bough, Billy watched while the helicopter gently lowered Durga's cage almost to the ground. Radar whispered something to Durga, opened the latch on the cage and dashed over to scramble up the tree. Durga paused for a moment as if to let Radar out of her way, sniffing the air and turning her head from side to side, from the temple ruins to the dark interior of the jungle. Then, with a graceful leap, she found her way back to freedom and to the home that welcomed her back.

The helicopter rose and disappeared from the scene. Billy and Radar were left with the sounds of the jungle and Durga, bemused and expectant as she reacquainted herself with the scent of the monsoon forest, the feeling of soft springy grass beneath her paws and the intense jewelled colours of the jungle.

Minutes passed. Concentrated minutes that went in slow motion. Then Durga stood still. A soft, low purring sound echoed around the clearing. It was a sound that hung suspended in the heavy air, with the vines and creeping plants. After each purr, Durga stopped and listened. And finally, the answer came: two answers to be exact, two high pitched versions of the same purr.

'Billy – look – over at the staircase straight ahead!' Radar whispered.

Billy gazed ahead. Something moved by the door at the top of the overgrown staircase of the temple. He could just make out two stripy faces peeking out from behind one of the sentinel stone tigers.

'Rani and Rajah!' gasped Radar.

Durga crept across the floor of the forest, slowly at first and then in huge bounds over the fallen mossy pillars. She reached the bottom of the old staircase. The air was filled with purrs and squeals of joy as the two little cubs leapt down onto their mother in a licking, boxing and nuzzling bundle of stripy joy.

'Wow…cool!' Billy was totally captivated by the tiger family. Slowly, Durga, Rani and Rajah came out from behind the ruins into the clearing and rolled and wrestled and cuddled to the power of ten.

'I bet Rani and Rajah thought they'd seen the last of their mother,' Radar looked down at the happy bundles of fur. 'Of course, the cubs are almost old enough to fend for themselves – they may have survived – but there's no replacing a mother. And to think what might have happened to her if those inhuman beasts had had their way…' He shuddered.

'I still wonder why Uncle Johnny let that creep Featherstonehaugh go. I wouldn't have – no way!' Billy was indignant.

'Oh well. Maybe the mud men got him. Or the crocodiles,' Radar grinned.

'Are there *really* crocodiles in that lake?'

'*Crocodilius*' natural habitat is fresh water and swamp in most regions of South East Asia…so make up your own mind.'

'You might have told me!'

Billy and Radar lolled in the branches of the huge exotic tree, watching the tigers play and then eventually stand up and lope into the forest behind the ruins, in search of something to eat. Before they disappeared from view, Durga turned back and let out a light growl to the boys.

'Goodbye Durga,' breathed Billy as Radar mouthed his own tiger farewell.

No sooner were the tigers out of sight than the buzz of the Whirlwind became audible above the background sound of the jungle. The boys scrambled back down the tree and waited in the clearing until the ladder dropped down from the helicopter. They both clambered up.

'Mission accomplished?' Grandpop grinned.

'Absolutely! Big cats re-grouped successfully.' Billy saluted. Grandpop and Radar laughed.

By the time they got back to RAF Botawaddy, the sun was beginning to set. The sweet smell of the jungle twilight met them as they climbed out of the Whirlwind onto the runway.

'We're going to have a bit of a bash in the Officers' Mess tonight in your honour. NCOs, other ranks and young scallywags most welcome. We'll leave our friend Kwok in his cell, though. Don't want him gobbling all our nosh. Twenty hundred sharp, then.' And Grandpop marched smartly away towards his quarters.

After a quick shower and change, the boys strolled across the compound, bathed in dusty twilight and gently buzzing with the sound of cicadas, to the Officers' Mess. Inside, Grandpop and Flt Sgt Singh, who were enjoying a pre-dinner gin and tonic, greeted them.

'Come and sit at the bar, you two young heroes. The chaps that arrived from Blighty this afternoon won't know what to do with themselves now. You've practically done their job for them! I think that two shandies are definitely in order.' Billy and Radar climbed up on the barstools and glanced around the Mess. Officers, some of whom Billy recognised from the briefing at Bigglesbrook all that time ago, and other ranks, were drinking, smoking and playing billiards but everyone gave a short nod or wave to the boys. After a while, the door opened and the Mess fell silent: the CO had arrived. An impressive-looking man with a big moustache, he walked over to the bar. Billy, Radar and the two men climbed respectfully down from their barstools.

'Normally,' the CO addressed Grandpop as much as the boys. 'Normally, I take a rather dim view of civilians getting involved in Squadron business. Particularly minors. But in this case, I have to say that Squadron Leader Walker convinced me and for that, I am grateful. All that remains to say on the matter is – to Flt Sgt Singh's ingenuity, to Squadron Leader Walker's resourcefulness and to the sheer damned bravery of these two young chaps – jolly good show!'

There was clapping and a chorus of "hear, hear!"s as several of the squadron came to congratulate the boys personally. Billy had never in his life had quite so many hearty pats on the back. On a couple of occasions he nearly choked on his shandy.

As darkness descended outside, they sat down to dinner. Menu cards with the Squadron's Crest and the date, 24th June 1962, stood at each place. Billy munched his way non-stop through Tomato Soup, Roast Chicken and Sherry Trifle until he couldn't eat any more. The dinner was accompanied by all manner of toasts, speeches and jokes that he didn't quite get but never mind. As the evening went on, he began to feel quite light-headed. He had vague impressions of young officers regressing under the influence of alcohol and playing polo on chairs with dessertspoons and oranges.

Billy also listened in on Grandpop's conversation with the CO regarding the Sunderland. She would be properly pensioned off, following her adventure. Next week, Grandpop would fly her to Bombay, where she would spend the rest of her days in a museum. But the most exciting thing was that

Grandpop would take the boys with him! Radar was due back at school and Billy would return to England:

'Best to get the old girl to a place of safety before anyone else "borrows" her! And there aren't many blighters left who were trained on that sort of kite,' Grandpop said. 'It will be a flight of some historical significance. *And* we'll make it back to Blighty in good time for the Bigglesbrook Air Fair!'

Both Billy and Radar were thrilled by the prospect and went to bed bubbling with renewed excitement and – it must be said – just a little bit tipsy.

Chapter 13

Senior Service

The remaining days at RAF Botawaddy were carefree and relaxed. Billy and Radar literally hung out in the monkey-puzzle tree house, recalling their adventures, which became more and more exaggerated with repeated telling. In the end, Billy couldn't say which bits were reality and which were merely figments of his imagination – or Radar's:

'I didn't want to tell you at the time, but when we were hanging over the side of the boat, I did actually see a crocodile basking in the shallows just a few feet away from us...I was praying that there wouldn't be blood spilt for him to smell...'

'...And when Featherstonehaugh had me by the neck, there was a moment when I totally stopped breathing...'

'...It was the toughest thing I've ever had to do – to stop Durga going for Kwok's jugular. But I had to think of Mani...'

'...That Indian cobra's forked tongue was *this close* to my face!'

'...And there really is poison in those darts that Mani's tribe use. Deadly poison that can finish you off in less than an hour...'

'...I dunno where I got the strength to hang onto the controls on the Sunderland. I thought we were all going to take a dive...'

When the day came to fly to Bombay, Grandpop, Radar and Billy bade goodbye to Flt Sgt Singh and RAF Botawaddy. As they left, Billy noticed Flt Sgt Singh surreptitiously slipping a package into Grandpop's hand and whispering to him. Singh seemed to sense that he was being watched and looked up. Billy met the dark mysterious smile of his friend's father and, for an instant, thought of home, and Gran, and half term. But these thoughts soon dissolved into the brilliant tropical sunshine as he marched with Radar, Grandpop and the rest of the crew to the lagoon. Radar was dressed in his school uniform with his hair slicked down. He dragged a huge trunk stamped with his initials "A.P.J.S." behind him.

At the lagoon, Billy gasped: under palms, off the end of a wooden jetty, the Sunderland bobbed at her mooring on bright turquoise water, peaceful after her dramatic adventure.

There was a crew of eight: Grandpop, the co-pilot, the navigator and three airmen, who would join the radio operator and the engineer who'd spent the night on board. They walked down the jetty and boarded a small launch to take them to the plane.

'Steady on with that trunk, shipmate,' yelled Grandpop as one of the crew members got rather over-enthusiastic with swinging Radar's trunk from launch to flying boat.

'Aye, aye, Captain!' returned the airman. Grandpop and the crew had slipped effortlessly from RAF to Senior Service slang in a continual stream of nautical banter.

'The end of an era,' Grandpop patted the fuselage as they climbed into the flying boat. 'And to think the rest of these have all ended up as frying pans. Thank God we managed to keep our hands on this one, even if Featherstonehaugh had other ideas!'

The flight would take six hours and they were starting early enough in the morning to avoid the worst of the monsoon. The navigator showed the boys the planned route and everyone took their seats ready for take-off. This was amazing: none of the hardness of wheels on concrete, just the feeling of being cushioned, first by softly breaking waves, then by air pockets in the cloudless sky. They rose above the sea. The palms and huts of RAF Botawaddy dwindled and finally disappeared from view as the Sunderland flew away from Burmeon and out over the wide ocean.

Later on, Billy and Radar sat on the bunks:

'What about playing Battleships?' Radar suggested. 'It'll be extra exciting being so close to a real ocean…any pens or paper around?'

'Hold on – I'll just look in this drawer here…' Billy pulled open a dark wooden drawer and grabbed a pile of paper. 'Oh, look – one of old Fanny's fag packets, "Senior Service" – empty, luckily. Hang on – he's written something on it. Here, Radar – there's a time and a date: 15:00, 8th July – that's next week, isn't it? And some letters, and a number, XM119…'

'Eaten by crocodiles or not, I don't trust Fanny one inch…'

'Me neither…'

Billy and Radar scrambled up to the cockpit with the cigarette packet. As Grandpop looked at it, the easy smile disappeared. His fists clenched:

'Damn him, damn him, damn him!'

'But, um…what does it mean? That's next week…oh, no! It's not the date of the…?'

'Exactly.' Grandpop confirmed Billy's worst suspicion. 'The Bigglesbrook Air Fair…and XM119 is the kite I'm due to fly in the formation display – the Hunter! If Fanny's mind works the way I think it does, this could kill or maim me and

God knows how many innocent bystanders. And destroy the reputation of the RAF!'

'D'you really think he was planning to nobble your plane, Squadron Leader? But we don't know if he's dead or alive...'

'With Fanny, you can't take chances.' Grandpop replied, grimly.

Billy's mind was ticking. Grandpop only died twelve years ago, so surely...but how *did* all this time business work, anyway? He remembered the date on the paper in the Lupin Tea Rooms and... no! The sabotaged car! Bigglesbrook – the microphone, the bugging. And someone in flying overalls walking towards...

'Uncle Johnny! He might already have done it! When I came out of the briefing...'

As Billy explained, concern and determination replaced the anger on Grandpop's face. There was no time to lose. The potential horror of the situation hit Billy like a revolver shot, shattering into a multitude of dreadful possibilities – and in this low-tech world, they were helpless to stop it:

'But, Uncle Johnny, can't you radio or something to get a message to them? I mean, what if someone wants to test-fly the Hunter...'

'Look, old chap. Nothing has happened yet. Getting us safely landed at Bombay is my first priority. Once we're there I'll need to get a cable out straight away. But first things first…'

What should have been a relaxed farewell turned into a crisis. Billy and Radar were left to find their way to the station as Grandpop dashed off in all urgency to embassies and telegraph offices. A cable to Bigglesbrook was vital, warning that absolutely no-one should touch Hunter XM119 until his return. Not only the reputation of the RAF, but innocent lives had to be protected at all costs. The impact of a disaster at the first Bigglesbrook Air Fair was unthinkable.

Billy couldn't help feeling sad on top of his anxiety about the Hunter, and Grandpop, and the Air Fair. He stood on a dusty railway platform in Bombay, saying his goodbyes to Radar. They'd been through so much together and now it had all come to an end. Radar's expression was serious and deep in thought. He was focussed on his school trunk, perched on a station trolley in front of him.

The train steamed in. And then Radar looked straight at Billy and grinned in that very knowing way that he had:

'Oh, you'll be seeing me very soon, old chum!'

Chapter 14

For your first-born

'Billy! We've got to scramble. Now!' The train had barely puffed away into the dusty distance when Billy was hurled back into the here-and-now by Grandpop's voice. 'Come on, old chap,' Grandpop clapped a reassuring hand on Billy's shoulder and marched him to the front of the station and into a waiting yellow-roofed taxi. 'Bit of a technical hitch, I'm afraid. Monsoon got slightly out of hand so the cables are all down. Tomorrow's a national holiday so there won't be anything doing then except some massive jamboree...yes, please...to Santa Cruz...and step on it, if you'd be so kind...'

The taxi swerved dangerously close to a scooter pulling a trailer piled high with watermelons. 'I got through to Singh at Botawaddy but the line went dead on me...' Grandpop yelled over the incessant hooting of the Bombay traffic '...nothing left but to get us on a commercial flight back to Blighty asap...'

They rushed through the terminal building with no time for food, or drink, or thought. Billy felt sticky and dusty and desperate for something cold and refreshing as they boarded the VC 10. How many hours had this taken last time? Almost a whole day and night, wasn't it? Twenty-four hours of worrying about whether they'd make it back in time...

As they flew westwards into the night, Grandpop settled back in his seat. 'Try to get some shut-eye if you can,' he said. 'We're going to need to be on the ball tomorrow.'

But sleep eluded Billy. Wild thoughts raced around his mind like a crazed flying formation. He tried to distract himself by taking advantage of everything offered to him by the flight crew: boiled sweets, pillows, blankets, hot towels and a rather good three-course dinner.

Grandpop spent most of the flight muttering in his sleep. It sounded as if he was re-enacting his showdown with Featherstonehaugh aboard the Sunderland – or a showdown yet to come. Billy opened a packet of salted peanuts and gazed out of the window. After a while, a thought occurred to him and he reached for his rucksack. Inside it was Mum's camera. He glanced idly at the photos of the lock in the dungeon and then took a couple more, one of Grandpop's travel bag, with the mysterious package that Flt Sgt Singh had handed him tucked into the side and one of the sleeping but restless Grandpop.

Billy's nose twitched at the reek of aircraft fuel and he shivered in the morning breeze. He loped down the steps after Grandpop and onto the airport runway.

'Well, here we are, old chap. Back in Blighty and a fine summer day it is, too. Good to be out of all that sweaty monsoon business – but we need to get going. First thing on the agenda is a reccy on XM119!'

Billy had to run to keep up with Grandpop as he marched through the terminal and straight into a cab. As they were driven back to Bigglesbrook, Grandpop explained his plan:

'Now, I don't think we'll make a big song-and-dance about this – until we know the score. Just slip in at the side entrance and make sure all is A-OK.'

Billy couldn't hear Grandpop's quiet but urgent words to the young guard on duty, but they were waved through. The car stopped by a hangar. Grandpop summoned a mechanic. Billy waited and watched, a feeling of lack of sleep and unease sweeping through his body. In the distance, Grandpop and the mechanic clambered over the Hunter. There was pointing, head scratching, dismantling of engine parts. A serious conversation in the corner. Head-nodding. Finally, Grandpop returned, wiping his hands on an oily cloth.

'Well, old chap, I think I can safely say that the entire RAF have you to thank for nipping a catastrophe in the bud. And you've probably saved my life...' Grandpop paused, smiling a smile that said everything, '...when I called Flight from Bombay, he told me the quickest way to nobble a Hunter. Minimum effort for maximum effect...'

'You mean Featherstonehaugh had already...'

'He certainly had, so damned well spotted – Good God! That could have been my last flight in more ways than one. I really do shudder to think...' he shook his head, teeth gritted. 'Nor can I write off the possibility of him escaping the crocodiles and Mani's chums – as I said, he's got it in for me – but I will be keeping a thorough personal check on this kite right up to the 8th July...'

'You *will* be careful, Grandpop...'

Grandpop ruffled Billy's hair. 'My own grandson, telling me to be careful? Hmph! I'd love to let you get the full glory for this...but it is a touch difficult – we don't want too many questions asked about you...'

Back at the Mess, Grandpop and Billy were greeted by an ecstatic Monty, all tongue and paws, jumping like hot popcorn as he saw them arrive. There was also an impressed-looking welcome party of officers who had heard about the triple-triumph of recovering the Sunderland, freeing Durga and capturing General Kwok, with minimum loss of life to man or beast. But, after the celebratory pink gins, ginger beers, cigars and sherbet fountains, Grandpop thanked his colleagues and nodded at Billy:

'If you'll excuse us, chaps, we need to retire to the terrace. We've got to think about getting the young nipper here back to...well, where he belongs. Come on, Billy.'

Billy and Grandpop wandered out through the elegant white-painted French windows to a shady terrace outside, followed by a bouncy Monty, who ran off onto the immaculately stripy lawn to chase butterflies. Billy lowered himself into a huge wicker chair and gazed out at the summer garden, drinking in the smell of lavender, the buzz of the bees, the feel of a gentle breeze on his bare arms. It was all very different to the tropical closeness of Burmeon. And finally, he voiced the thought that he'd had no time to think about. But a thought that had been constantly there, lurking, like a crocodile:

'Grandpop? How *are* you going to get me back to Gran?'

Grandpop puffed on his pipe thoughtfully and glanced up at a Chipmunk dancing across the forget-me-not blue sky. 'I told you we'd find a way…something is bound to turn up. In the meantime, what do you say to having a reccy of that package that Flight gave me? He was most insistent that I didn't open it until we got back to Blighty…seems like now is as good a time as any…'

When Grandpop returned with the package, Billy was bursting with excitement. He could still see the mysterious look that Flt Sgt Singh had given him on that last sunny day in RAF Botawaddy.

'Now, steady on, steady on!' Grandpop grinned as Billy craned his neck to see the package and Monty bounded up to join in the fun. 'First of all, there's a little card here.' He held up a card with the Squadron crest: 'to your first-born, for saving my first-born. Respectfully Yours, Prabhakar A.J.Singh.' Grandpop wrinkled his brow. 'What the heck does he mean by that, the old devil? My first-born isn't, yet, as it were, and *his* first-born…'

'…Is Radar!' Billy cried excitedly. 'It's a thank you…to you…and *your* first-born is my mum…so it must be sort of for me, too!'

'Well, you'd better get cracking and open it, then!' Grandpop smiled and handed the package to Billy, who couldn't wait to tear into it. Under the brown paper was a board box, with a marbled pattern in deep indigoes and emerald greens. The box had a little metal clip and Billy's fingers suddenly felt super-clumsy as he fiddled to open it.

Billy gasped when he saw what was inside. His hands automatically fell to his sides and he gazed down at the contents in a mixture of awe and thankfulness.

'Oh, wow!' It was all he could say.

Lying in the box, on a bed of blue velvet was the silver kaleidoscope, with its engraving of what Billy now knew to be the goddess Durga, riding on a tiger. Grandpop peered into the box to see what all the fuss was about. 'Great Scott! It's your time-travel-tube jobby!' Billy picked it up, cautiously, as if it was made from delicate crystal. He didn't dare start looking into it. Now that he knew its power, he was amazed at the reckless way that he'd played around with the thing all that time ago in Mum's old bedroom.

'There's a note here, from Singh...' Grandpop was saying '...the goddess Durga...he says it's mostly glass inside but that you may just catch a glimpse of a ruby...and so on and so forth...but, old chap...I take it you know what this means?'

Billy looked into Grandpop's sky-blue eyes, serious for once. He felt torn: blissfully happy and achingly sad all at the same time. 'Yes, Grandpop. I do.'

Neither of them said what didn't actually need to be said. Practical as ever, Grandpop began planning the next move:

'Now, I don't profess to be much of a boffin – that's always been Flight's department – but what knowledge of orienteering I possess says if in doubt, go back to start...how does that sound to you?'

'Well, yeah. I suppose if I'm going to do it, I ought to do it there. By the Forget-me-not Stores.'

'Good. That's sorted. And I can pay the old girl – er, your grandmother – a surprise visit when we've got you back! She's not actually expecting me for another two days! So...let's get Monty and get going. Not forgetting your knapsack or this splendid kaleidoscope, of course. I wonder how the motor's feeling today.'

Billy, Monty and Grandpop hopped into the little frog-eyed car, which started with its familiar *pfft pfft pfft*. And they were off, back into the English countryside: the hedgerows sprinkled with dog roses, the narrow curving roads, the ancient oaks with deep green leaves and the rolling fields of grain, turning from green to gold, blowing in the breeze.

Billy leaned back, shut his eyes and dozed. Scenes from his adventures mixed up in his mind. General Kwok, stranded in a bark canoe; Mani, driving the steam train into Bombay station; Monty bouncing and barking through the ruined temple; Flt Sgt Singh, astride a BSA motorbike, jumping a hump-backed bridge; Durga, Rani and Rajah sitting at the bar in RAF Botawaddy, drinking pink gin…

When he woke up, Billy felt odd. Strangely enough, odder than he had felt the whole way through, from the first moment that he had conjured up Grandpop in Gran's house. It was the oddness that comes from knowing. Knowing that he had gone back in time and knowing that he now had the means to go forward again. But Grandpop was treating the whole thing like just another job to be done: he puffed his pipe as he drove and occasionally swept his hair out of his eyes where it had flopped down. Billy turned his attention to the glorious countryside outside.

Gradually, the lanes and villages took on a more familiar air. Billy had a growing feeling that he knew where he was, although maybe he just recognised these places from their journey to Bigglesbrook. In one case, that was certain: they stopped by the Lupin Tea Rooms to fill up at the National Benzole filling station. But, as they drove on Billy saw more and more houses, roads, bridges, corners and place names that he knew.

As they motored down a straight, sunlit road, with large houses hidden in tree-lined sprawling gardens on each side, Billy knew exactly where he was. But it was all so different: the road-signs were fewer and quainter, the road markings as good as non-existent. And the other road users were more individual and more polite: a motorbike with sidecar, a green delivery van with elegant gold lettering and brightly coloured cars with chrome headlights and radiators like faces. Everything was calmer, sunnier and more solid, somehow.

Suddenly, Billy's oddness turned into full-blown panic:

'Grandpop? Do I really have to go back? Can't I stay here with you?' He felt overwhelmed with confused sadness.

'Chin up, old chap. What about your chums at school? What about Mum and Dad? Or Gran? No point in hanging around with an old buffer like me now that we've done our job and found how to get you back. Or forward.'

Billy's mind lurched back into neutral and he reached for Monty's reassuring warmth. The little dog gave him a playful lick on the cheek as if he understood.

The Austin Healey turned into a bumpy sandy lane and Grandpop parked in front of the Forget-me-not Stores. A Wall's Ice Cream banner flapped in the summer breeze.

'Well, the time has come, as the walrus said...I suggest you make it snappy: I know that I'm not too keen on long goodbyes, and I reckon you aren't, either...'

Billy smiled, gave Monty a big cuddle and turned to Grandpop:

'Grandpop...that was all...wizard!' Grandpop grinned and passed Billy the kaleidoscope, like a relay baton. Billy looked into Grandpop's brave and cheery blue eyes for the last time.

'Cheerio, then, old chap!' Billy felt Grandpop ruffle his hair as he put the kaleidoscope to his eye. He twisted the cylinder cautiously at first, then with more purpose as he gradually slipped away from that lazy July afternoon in 1962. Grandpop's pipe smoke became a mere hint on the breeze and Monty's yaps faded into the distance as Billy's entire consciousness tumbled into a tunnel of dislocated sights, sounds and smells. And suddenly, familiar but uninvited sensations barged into Billy's world, like gatecrashers at a party: the whiff of plasticky cheeseburgers, the jangle of ring tones, the garish fuchsia pinks and puke purples of a kiddies' pony roundabout.

Billy was standing in the car park of Tesbury's supermarket. His head was reeling. All around him, there was simply too much going on. To the left, a harassed mother with three little girls in grubby pink, trying to find the right sort of trolley from the twenty or so on offer. To the right, an unnaturally tanned woman in a giant tank of a 4X4 trying to squeeze into a parking place while squeaking and squealing at someone or something on her mobile phone. Ahead, a group of overweight teenage boys with trousers at half-mast waddled by, mouths wrapped around double quarter-pounders oozing tomato ketchup.

Billy shut his eyes for a moment, felt for his rucksack, then shrugged his shoulders and walked away from Tesbury's in a daze, puzzled as to why on earth he had landed here of all places. But one thing was certain: he was back in the 21st century world of rushing, dashing and flapping continuously and purposelessly. Everyone was in his or her bubble of pointless activity and it was probably of no concern to anyone that a boy had just appeared in their midst, fresh from the last century. There was no one around who was in the faintest bit interested in Billy Blake. For the first time in what seemed like weeks, he was alone. It was a feeling that he had to get used to again. Billy, alone in his own little world, lost in a dream as he wandered through the sunlit streets that led back to Gran's.

Gran's road was one that didn't really go anywhere except to the houses there. It was a like a relic from the past: here there were also few road markings. A sign saying "Unadopted" hung under the road sign. Billy turned into Gran's unadopted road, where there were no pavements, and looked at his watch. It was a quarter to three. He reached the bend in the road and saw Gran's house in front of him, white and welcoming, surrounded by the dark green and crimson of the rhododendrons. He felt a real longing not to be alone any more – to see Gran, or Mum and Dad, or George or any of his friends from school. Not that he wanted to tell everyone about Grandpop and his adventures – that was his special secret. But he had a desperate yearning for company and the normality of everyday life.

Listening to his lone footsteps, he walked into the driveway of *Pinemount*. Gran's car was not parked in the drive; she must still be at the church. For Billy, the recent past had focussed on Gran, and being in this house, in looking through the toy box and in glancing out onto the lawn on a summer night. It really didn't seem so long ago that he had been looking into the kaleidoscope in Mum's old room, trying to summon up Grandpop for a second time. What had happened in between had moved to a different place in his memory – a place where dreams and stories are kept.

He sat down on the bench in the porch. Not quite knowing what to expect, he took his mother's camera out of his rucksack and switched it onto playback mode. In the cool and shade of the porch, he flicked through. Nothing. No photos of locks or dungeons and no shots of the inside of a 1962 VC 10 or a sleeping Grandpop. They were all gone, lost in another world. As Billy put the camera back in his rucksack, puzzled but not upset, Gran's little green hatchback drew up on the gravel drive.

'Hello Billy! How sweet of you to sit there and wait for me! I hope you managed to amuse yourself while I was away…'

'Oh, I did Gran. No problem! What's for tea today?'

'Well, do you know, I dropped by at Tesbury's on the way back and they just happened to have some tins of Peek Frean's Afternoon Tea Assorted – it was something called a

"Nostalgia Biscuit Tin Promotion" – and while I'm not sure about being a piece of nostalgia, I bought them anyway. They were always Johnny's favourites. He told me once that he couldn't live without them!'

A few days later, Billy and Gran were enjoying a cup of tea and some Peek Frean's biscuits in the cool of Gran's sitting room as the late afternoon sun blazed through the fir trees. Billy found it quite odd to see the biscuit tin, sitting so primly amongst Gran's porcelain tea service, instead of wrapped up in oilskins or in a dusty tunnel, primed to explode. He glanced across at the black and white portrait photo of Grandpop on the mantelpiece. Since his adventures, all the photos of Grandpop or planes in the house had taken on a new meaning, or one could say, a life of their own. Billy could almost see those eyes twinkling blue under the RAF cap; he could almost hear Grandpop's voice...

'Gran,' he asked. 'Why did Grandpop die?'

Gran was taken aback, but she shook her head slightly and smiled:

'What a very strange question, Billy. Why? I've often asked myself. *How* is clear enough. His heart...stopped. But why? You know, Billy, sometimes I think that Johnny didn't really fit in this modern world. Or rather, it didn't fit him. Your Grandpop was a gentleman, Billy. He could see his world slipping away from him. Everything he held dear seemed to be less and less relevant to almost everybody else. So he wanted to take his leave. To do the decent thing and make place for the young chaps, he would have said. And, in the end, he found a way. He knew, somehow, that his time was done.' Gran paused and took a sip of tea. Was that it? Billy desperately wanted to hear more. He was on the point of asking, trying to find the right words, when Gran continued:

'It was our wedding anniversary. He took me up flying in a light aircraft at the aerodrome. We had a glorious time but suddenly Johnny started feeling unwell. He managed to land safely but he collapsed as he left the aircraft. Later that evening, he flew west, as they say.'

'Poor Gran,' Billy could see tears in the old lady's eyes.

'Oh, I'm not poor, Billy!' Gran smiled through. 'Goodness me. I'm not poor at all! I was married to him for over forty years…and, now that he's gone, I carry on regardless, as Johnny used to say. With my memories. So many wonderful memories! I'll never forget the day your Mum was born…when Johnny rushed back from the Bigglesbrook Air Fair – it was the first one ever – to see his new baby daughter.

I'll swear he drove that car faster than he flew in the Hunter that day! No, not a single minute of a single day goes by when I don't think about him.'

'You must miss him so much.'

'I do, Billy, I do. I miss him terribly. But, do you know? It may sound silly, but...' and Gran's voice brightened, 'there really are times when I feel as if he is very, very close.' She smiled and gazed at the photo.

'I miss him, too,' Billy said, quietly.

Gran turned her gaze from the photo to Billy and smiled:

'You understand, don't you?'

Billy nodded.

Chapter 15

Ajay

Back at school, Josh was wild with stories to tell about the half-term holidays. This always happened and usually took up at least the first day back. Josh had been to Granddad "Call-me-Les" and Nan's place in the Algarve. At first, it seemed as if the whole performance would be the same as usual. From his place in the classroom, a couple of rows back from Josh and his audience, Billy could hear tales of the quad bike, the jacuzzi and the Home Cinema.

But there was something unusual this time; it was clear that the other boys were not as enthralled by Josh's tales of his granddad's luxury lifestyle as they had been before. No, every now and then, a boy would come up to the crowd with a story thousands of times more gripping:

'Never mind that: did you see it last night? Wasn't that just awesome!'

'Yeah, yeah…where he was dropped by parachute into that creepy old temple…'

'And he was right in whisker's length of that tiger…wicked, or what?'

'Didn't you see it, Josh? It nearly did my head in. Ajay. Talking with tigers...mega-cool!'

And Josh, realising that Call-me-Les's toys were no match for a man who could talk with tigers, resorted to a bit of Billy-baiting as a distraction manoeuvre:

'Brain of a flea, brain of a pea

Billy Blake's got ADD.'

But Billy, who was staring out of the window – what else? – didn't care. He too had seen Ajay's Adventures last night. And if there had been any tiny doubt in his mind about whether it had all really happened, somewhere, sometime – Grandpop, Burmeon, Durga and Radar - the first shot of Ajay as he prepared to parachute out of the helicopter to discover the tigers of the Democratic Republic of Ybur wiped it away. His hair was grey but his eyes still burned passionately for nature and the wonders of the world as he found Rajah and Rani's grandchildren, still living in the ruins of the old temple. And, as the closing credits came up: "Ajay's Adventures was conceived and directed by Ajay Singh, Fellow of the Royal Geographic Society," he felt as if he'd known all along.

Billy gazed out of the classroom window, smiling, lost in a dream.

~ The End ~

Glossary of RAF terms & slang

Angel: one angel = one thousand feet altitude

Blighty: Britain

BOAC: British Overseas Airways Corporation – the long-haul British state airline from 1946 to 1974

Boffin: scientist

Cab: helicopter/aircraft

Char: tea

Chopper: helicopter

CO: Commanding Officer

DC3: Douglas DC3, a cargo and passenger aircraft still in use today

Dickie seat: 2nd pilot's seat

Flight Sergeant: A senior non-commissioned rank in the RAF

Fly/flew west: die, died

Khazi: toilet

Kite: plane

NAAFI: Navy, Army & Air Force Institutes. Shops and other services for British servicemen, usually on military bases.

NCO: Non-commissioned officer – includes all ranks of corporals and sergeants

Senior Service: The Royal Navy, also a brand of cigarettes popular in the 1960s

Squadron Leader: A commissioned rank in the RAF, above Flight Lieutenant and below Wing Commander

~~~

www.burmeon.com

About The Author

Flying and travel are in Susan Moss's blood – she visited four of the world's continents before starting school. She read avidly and wrote determinedly in between plotting to become a spy and building brother-proof camps.

She studied Psychology at Trinity College, Cambridge, taking part in some interesting experiments in parapsychology as well as playing trumpet in a Big Band.

A chance meeting in an Austrian ski hut resulted in more travel – this time to Germany, where she now lives in a small town outside Frankfurt with her husband and son.

She still makes use of her trumpet-playing, spying and camp-building skills in her busy life as an author, mother and freelance marketing consultant.

The Bother in Burmeon is her first published novel.

More adventure fiction from Circaidy Gregory Press

Herm's Secret
by Kate O'Hearn

Come to Herm now, or you'll die!

Lori Watson is just a normal, 13-year-old girl until she hears the strange voice warning that her life is in danger. Her only chance of survival is to get to the tiny channel island of Herm, a remote, mist-shrouded place that holds the key to her true nature.

Gunrunners, kidnappers, and a fight for the survival of a rare species: her arrival on Herm is only the beginning of a terrifying ordeal that will change her life forever…

Herm's Secret £7.49
Paperback ISBN 978-1-906451-31-8
Ebook ISBN 978-1-906451-38-7
Order from www.circaidygregory.co.uk